Born and educated in Londc
steadily for the past thirty y
many translations and on co
has written widely on the hu
and is often consulted on tec
An ex-editor, E. C. Tubb co
Fiction Association; he won the short story award at the Trieste Festival and was chosen to be guest of honour at the World Science Fiction Convention at Heidelberg. His studies embrace astronomy, physics and extra-sensory perception while his hobbies include photography, ancient weapons and archaeology.

Also by E. C. Tubb:

SPACE 1999: BREAKAWAY
SPACE 1999: COLLISION COURSE
SPACE 1999: ALIEN SEED
SPACE 1999: ROGUE PLANET
SPACE 1999: EARTHFALL

E. C. Tubb

The Primitive

Futura Publications Limited
An Orbit Book

An Orbit Book

First published by Futura Publications
Limited in 1977

To: Jean and Daphne

ISBN 0 8600 7974 0
Printed in Great Britain by
Hazell Watson & Viney Ltd
Aylesbury, Bucks

Futura Publications Limited
110 Warner Road
Camberwell, London SE5

ONE

His name was Leon Vardis and he was nine when his mother died. He never knew his father who, he was given to understand, had died in some distant affray. He was a tall, well-formed boy with thick dark hair reaching to his shoulders, blue eyes deep-set beneath level brows, a firm chin and a mouth which was normally soft but which could be cruel at times of anger. Fatherless, he had quickly learned to rely on none, questing far into the northern hills in search of game, necessity making him adept with sling, bow and knife.

The summer had been hot, with searing winds and no rain, so that the crops stood weakly in the fields, the stalks brittle and the seed shrivelled in the ears. He had left early, moving in a wide sweep from the edge of his mother's holding to where a dry riverbed snaked up the rocky slopes. There could be snakes beneath the stones, or lizards, or other things containing meat and moisture. Noon found him high on the hills, his game-bag empty, ravenous and burning with thirst. Sitting, he drank from his canteen and ate a slice of rough bread smeared with a paste made of cockroaches and ants, dried, pounded and mixed with a little honey. Resting, he looked down at the village.

Weitonburg was a small place. A cluster of buildings stood at the crossroads; a meeting hall which also served as a church and council chamber, schoolroom and courthouse. A tavern, forge, tanning yard and general store. To one side reared the communal granaries, the livestock pens and a carpenter's yard. Around them, smaller houses built of wood and stone housed the elite of the community. Further out, standing alone in dusty fields, a straggle of lesser dwellings belonged to those who worked their own land. Leon had good eyes. From where he sat he could see tiny figures, like ants, moving restlessly about the centre of the village. From the south, a cloud of dust rose from beneath the hooves of a solitary horseman heading towards the community. The regular, ten-day messenger, from Elkton, perhaps. It could hardly have been a casual traveller.

Rising, he continued his hunt, pressing higher and deeper into the hills, following a narrow gulley and losing sight of the village. He collected a mass of beetles which he placed in a tin, a double-handful of grass seeds and a few edible roots, withered by lack of moisture but still containing starch and flavour. Rounding a boulder, he caught a glimpse of movement, and froze as he saw the lizard. It was a big one, almost two feet from snout to tail, food for at least two days. Cautiously, he studied the terrain.

To advance would be to frighten the beast, to move too quickly the same. It rested on the summit of a rock, head towards a patch of shadow cast by a spined bush, good cover if it should decide to run. Leon backed, slowly, bare feet silent on the sun-heated stone. Out of sight, he climbed so as to get above and beyond his prey, dropping down to attack it from the other side. His sling would make too much noise at such close quarters. His bow was light, the arrows crude, good enough to kill unarmoured game but doubtful against the lizard, unless he could hit the tiny target of an eye. Stooping, he picked up a large stone. If he could throw it hard enough and accurately enough he would knock the creature from the rock, stun it perhaps, leave it to squirm while he gashed the throat and belly with his knife. As he shifted his feet, arm poised to throw the stone, the ground fell away from beneath his feet.

It was a pit some fifteen feet deep, the sides smooth and narrowing as they reared towards the surface, where a thin crust of soil had been left to trap the unwary. The air was dank and held a foetid odour. To one side, an opening about two feet wide made a dark patch against the sunlight streaming through the ragged opening above. Close to it, the odour was stronger, a sharp, acrid, insect smell and the edge was scored with the thin gouges of scrabbling limbs.

Leon backed, swallowing, his body oozing the sweat of fear. For the moment he was safe, the brilliant sunlight would keep the creature at bay, but when darkness fell it would emerge to feast, later climbing the walls of its pit to restore the skin of surface dirt with saliva-cemented soil.

Desperately he examined his prison. The pit was six feet wide at the bottom, far too wide for him to straddle, narrowing to half as much at the surface. He had fallen heavily, smashing his bow, and bruising side and shoulder. The arrows would be of no use against the armoured thing lurking in the side opening, his sling little better. He had his knife, and the stone he'd intended to use against the lizard. Neither would be of much use when it grew dark.

Uneasily he glanced at the opening above. Already the sun had moved across the sky so that the lower reaches of the pit were thick with shadows. From the opening came a scraping sound, and a waft of stench clogged his nostrils. The thing was hungry and getting impatient. There was no time to lose.

Grimly Leon attacked the side of the pit, stabbing at the smoothed soil with his knife, gouging foot and handholes in the gritty surface. He worked to one side of the opening, sending little showers of loosened soil over his head and back, blinking as, back arched, he slowly mounted. It took a long time. Several times he had to stop, climbing down to ease his aching muscles, uneasily aware of the stirrings of the thing in its lair. When he finally reached the opening, it was dusk, thick shadows filling the pit and only a diffused glow illuminating the upper portions.

As he dug the last handhold the thing emerged from its nest.

He heard the scrape of something large, a thin chittering, a scrabbling, and choked in an almost overpowering reek. Frantically he slammed the blade deep into the crumbling soil, heaved, managed to get his free hand on the ragged edge of the opening. Dirt showered on head and shoulders as his weight tore at the earth. He fell, hanging suspended by his grip on the knife, while below him a black shape rushed furiously upwards.

Fear spurred his flagging strength. With a convulsive jerk he heaved upwards, found the edge again, lifted his other hand while his foot kicked against the hilt of the knife. Arms and chest beyond the edge of the pit he kicked, screamed as he felt something tear at his leg, kicked again with frantic terror. Thorns tore at his hand as he gripped a branch and pulled, stones ripping his skin as he rolled desperately from the edge of the pit. Within the opening black limbs rose, spined, hooked, followed by the pincer-jaws and glittering eyes of the subterranean predator.

Gasping, retching from the stench of the thing, Leon ran back down the path he had taken. Blood shone red in the dying light as it dripped from his lacerated ankle, his torn hands and chest. Only when the danger was safely behind him did he dare to halt to examine his wounds. With his teeth he drew the thorns from his hand and then tore a strip of fabric from his kirtle to bandage his leg. The wounds were long, shallow, the flesh removed as if with a surgical instrument, burning like fire from the venom the creature had carried on its claws. Gritting his teeth, he stumbled on his way.

He saw the fire as he left the hills. It was quite dark, the moonless sky sprinkled with stars, and against the darkness the glow of the fire leapt with accentuated brilliance. He raced towards it, the pain of his wounds forgotten, heart hammering in his chest as he recognised the site of the blaze. It was his house that was burning, the shack in which he lived with his mother, gouts of flame leaping from the roof as the sun-dried timbers roared, sparks showering from writhing columns of smoke. The fire blinded him. He didn't see the shadow which rose to one side of the trail, the bulk of the body which snared him in its arms.

'What—?'

'Quiet, boy! Silent for your life!'

He twisted, recognising the face touched by the ruby glow. 'Grochen! Let me go! My mother—'

'—is dying!' The voice matched the man, hard, rough, aggressively strong. One big hand clamped across Leon's mouth as Grochen lifted him and carried him deep into the corn flanking the trail. Stalks snapped and rustled as they moved, the sounds lost in the roaring fury of the blaze, the maniacal yells of men bearing torches, the screaming of something lashed to a stake and wreathed in flame.

'Your mother,' said Grochen. His voice was strained like that of a man torn between tears and anger. 'I came visiting and she was worried at your absence. I went to look for you and was in the hills when they came. Then it was too late. All I could do was to wait for your return.'

Leon jerked, fighting the hand which was clamped on his mouth.

'Steady, lad!' Grochen held fast to the struggling boy. 'They'll kill you too, if they find you. I heard them talking; the witch and her spawn both, they said. That's why I waited for you. Now be still. There's nothing we can do.'

Nothing but watch his mother burn.

The night was old before they could move. A thin wind had risen from the east, stirring the ashes and filling the air with the stench of charring flesh. The men had gone, first to the tavern and then to their homes, using their women and then falling into heavy slumber. Like ghosts, Grochen and the boy made their way to the house of the Chief Elder, hugging shadows, pausing by the locked panel of the back door. There were dogs, but they knew Leon and allowed him to stroke their muzzles, dying beneath Grochen's blade before they could bark the alarm.

Gently Leon leaned against the panel, leaned and pushed, veins standing rigid against his throat and forehead, muscles taut, legs firm against the earth as he fought the bar within.

It yielded with a dull snap and they entered darkness. A curtain moved and starlight cast its eerie glow.

Grochen's voice was a whisper. 'Leon?'

'Upstairs.'

He led the way, heart pounding, mouth dry with anticipation. Only twice in his life had he entered Elder Philbart's house; once when Cylla, the daughter of Philbart's bondsmaid, had shown Leon the library of eighteen books, and once when the Provost had sent him with a message. The first time Cylla had led him, with the devilment of youth, upstairs to the master bedroom, the second he had only reached the entrance chamber; but that single time had been enough. He knew where the Elder would be sleeping.

He paused before the door and felt Grochen at his side. He had followed the big man from the fire, knowing, without the necessity of words, what had to be done. It was like a drug in his veins, so that every cell of his being quivered with a life of its own. There was sickness and there was horror but also there was a grim determination. Alone he could never have done it, but he was not alone.

'Now,' said Grochen, and thrust open the door.

The Elder was old and his sleep could not have been easy. He reared up in the wide bed, primitive warning widening his eyes, opening his mouth to summon aid. The cry died beneath the cover of Grochen's hand, that same hand pressing the figure back onto the bed, the head into the pillow.

'Now, boy,' he whispered. 'Now!'

Leon's hand fell from his empty sheath. 'My knife! I have no knife!'

'Use mine.' Grochen extended the hilt, the blade still wet with dogs' blood. 'Quickly!'

The hilt was big in his hand, the blade a curved and pointed instrument of death. He rested the point against the scrawny throat and pushed. The skin was tougher than he had imagined. The point drew a single drop of blood which welled from the skin around the steel.

Philbart heaved, his thin body arching from the bed, his eyes wild as they rolled in their sockets. His eyes shone, huge with terror, catching a glimmer of starlight from the curtains and reflecting it like flame.

Leon thrust at the blade, felt a resistance, a sudden yielding, saw the thick spurting which wet pillow and hand.

'For my mother,' he said. 'For the woman you allowed to be killed.'

And stepped back, sobbing for breath as he watched the old man die.

They left the house as they had entered, quietly, carrying a bundle of clothing, weapons, some articles of value, together with food and a flask of water and another of wine. Leon had wanted to fire the building to repay death and flames with more of the same, but Grochen had stopped him.

'No, lad, there is a better way.' He explained as they stood in the starlight. 'The whole village is guilty and the whole village should pay. Can you carry these things?'

The bundle was heavy, but Leon nodded.

'Good. Take the road to the east, but walk a hundred yards to the right. I shall follow you. If I am caught, get rid of what you carry and veer to the south. Enter the third village you find and tell them you are lost. Say nothing about the fire or what has happened here this night. Let the blame be mine. You understand?'

'Yes.' Leon looked at the big man. 'What do you intend to do?'

'Fire the granaries. Before spring all will face starvation. Now go!'

Leon picked up the bundle and moved to where thick shadow rested between two houses. Dropping it, he stole back and followed Grochen as he moved towards the granaries. From his belt he slipped his sling, fitting a stone as his eyes searched for the guards. There were two of them, Provost's men, wearing quilted armour and helmets of hammered iron, armed with sword, dagger and spear. A torch threw a flickering light over the door and the immediate surround of the building, touching the armoured men with moving patches of orange, yellow and crimson. One of them said something to his companion, who grunted, hefted his spear, and went to circle the building. As the guard passed from the patch of light Grochen staggered from the shadow of a building and moved towards the remaining guard.

He was obviously drunk. He fell twice each time rising unsteadily to his feet, each time coming a little closer to where the guard watched with cynical amusement.

'That's enough, fellow!' The spear lowered and rested level with Grochen's stomach. 'You've had your fun, but this is no place to sleep it off.'

Grochen paused, hands pawing the air. 'What's that you say?'

'Get moving!' The guard frowned. 'You're Grochen, aren't you? Another damned stranger. I—' The spear fell as he screamed and raised both hands to his face. From the socket of his left eye sprouted the hilt of a thrown dagger. As Grochen moved forward, Leon began to send his sling whipping through the air.

He was just in time. Attracted by the scream, the second guard came running towards the patch of light. He saw Grochen, halted and poised his spear. As his arm drew back for the throw, Leon released the sling, the stone whining through the air to smash against the side of the helmet. The man fell. Grochen rose, knife in hand, ran to the fallen guard and stabbed him in the throat. He turned once, lifting his hand, then vanished into the building, opening the locked door with a key he had found in the Elder's chamber.

He was inside for five minutes and then returned, running. To Leon he said, 'Where's the bundle?'

'Over there.' Leon pointed. 'In those shadows.'

Grochen picked it up and swung it over his shoulder. 'Right,' he said. 'Now let's get away from here.'

They watched the fire from the crest of the northern hills, leaning back, eating dried meat and fruits as the stars paled in the sky. Seeing the flames, Leon lost his appetite, thinking of another such fire, the sounds and smells of it, feeling for the first time an aching sense of loss.

'Mother' he said. 'Mother.'

'She was a good woman,' said Grochen heavily. 'A fine woman. She had the gift of healing and did more for me than a dozen doctors in a score of towns. She made me whole again, enabled me to walk without pain, showed me the joyful thing that life should be. I loved her, Leon. I would have married her any time she chose.'

Leon blinked the tears from his eyes. 'Why?' he demanded. 'Why did they kill her?'

'Because they are fools and afraid.' Grochen's voice thickened as he looked towards the blaze. 'The crops have failed, diseased in the fields, and the prospect of hunger drove them mad. A messenger arrived from Elkton with talk of a Cleansing, and is was like putting a match to hay. Your mother lived alone, without a man to protect her. She was a sensitive, and had a magic gift. And she was a stranger. She came to the village with you as a babe in her arms. She had no family and no kin. And so they burned her, may God rot their souls! They took that gentle woman and burned her!'

His voice was a cry of pain and for a long time he looked towards the rising sun. The east was bright but hardly bright enough to cause watering. Yet his eyes were moist when he looked again at the boy.

'You've killed,' he said. 'It was a thing which had to be done if ever you are to know rest, but the other thing belonged to me. I too had to make them pay. You understand?'

Leon wasn't sure. He had been swept along on a tide of events, reacting, rather than choosing his actions, doing what had to be done without conscious thought. Grochen was a friend, a regular visitor, and one who had helped him in many ways, but could he feel as close to the dead woman as the child of her body?

He moved, and involuntarily winced at the pain from his leg. Grochen pursed his lips as he examined the injury. 'A klarge in the hills? I thought we'd checked the area and burned them out. The damn things must be moving back towards the plain. You were lucky to escape.' He frowned and amended his statement. 'No, not lucky, clever. You used your head and so saved your life. I'm proud of you, Leon.'

His mother, too, would have been proud, had she been alive. His mother!

'Cry if you want to,' said Grochen. 'Get it out of your system.'

'No.' Leon firmed his lips. 'She's gone. I shall never forget her – but she's gone.' He looked at the distant column of smoke, at the waste all around, feeling very small and vulnerable. He was, aside, from Grochen, alone in a hostile world, and he realised how dependent he was on the man.

Sitting, easing his painful ankle, he looked at his companion. Grochen was big, that he had known, hard and rough in his worn clothing and scuffed boots. His face was seamed with time and weather, his hair cropped and his skull was glistening with the tissue of old scars. His hands matched his face, the knuckles swollen, the wrists thick – the hands of a worker or fighter. He lifted one to shade his eyes, squinting.

'Your eyes are younger than mine, Leon. Are those horsemen, leaving the village?'

'Yes. One on each road.'

'Damn!' Grochen lowered his hand, clenching it into a fist. 'The Provost is no fool. He's sending messengers all over the area and there'll be a reward for our capture. We'll have to avoid meeting anyone until we reach the coast. There are towns there and no one will worry about a couple of strangers.' He glanced at the bandaged ankle. 'How about that leg? Can you keep walking?'

'Yes,' said Leon.

He limped a little as they set off. The rest had stiffened the wounds, but he hoped the renewed exercise would restore his muscles to normal. The wound itself was inflamed, the flesh around it swollen and tender. Worriedly Grochen scratched at his stubbled chin.

'We need help Leon. The venom isn't dissipating, and you're going to get worse.'

'We could rest.' The thought of it filled the boy with longing. To sit down somewhere, to sprawl, to ease his burning skin with cool water and to have to do nothing but simply lie and sleep or look at the sky.

Grochen was curt. 'No. We've no water and little food and we aren't going to find either in this wilderness.' He pointed to where a road traced a path across an expanse of bleached grass, sun-scorched and withered. 'That road must lead to a village. We'll follow it and get help.'

'And be captured?'

'Maybe not,' said Grochen. 'Maybe not.'

The stolen food had included a few eggs pickled in their shells. One remained. He took it and carefully removed the shell and the thin layer of membrane within. With his knife he cut the skin into circles and, using the blade as a mirror, laid them over each eyeball. He stopped, rubbed grey dust on his face and hair, reached before him with trembling hands.

'Help me,' he quavered. 'Help a poor, blind old man. Help me.'

Leon stared at the milky orbs with horrified fascination. Coated by the thin skin they looked dead, lifeless. 'Can you see?'

'A little.' Grochen removed the membranes and blinked the moisture from his eyes. 'Enough to get by with, but I can't make out detail. It's a trick I learned as a boy on the Eintar Lakes. I had a master who forced me to beg, and most have pity for the blind.' He ripped spare clothing into strands and fashioned a noosed rope. The noose he dropped over Leon's head and set it snugly around his neck. 'You are lame and can barely speak, remember that. Talk only in grunts. A sharp stone beneath your tongue will help you to remember. I'm an old man, blind, and with a young idiot to guide me. Leave all the talking to me.' He twitched the rope. 'Let's practice a little before I put back the skins.'

They reached the village just before dusk, when the sun was low on the horizon; a lambent ball of orange flame set in a bowl of featureless green. It was a place much larger than Weitonburg, a Node-Village with a high stone wall set with watch towers, the wall pierced with arched gates and surrounded by a broad moat. The moat was dry now, even the bottom-weeds sere and brittle, the fish which had once finned among them long since gone. Neglected, too, were the walls which had once beaten back the attacks of men and voracious life forms, the stones cracked and mottled with lichen, stained by the frosts of a hundred winters and by the savage suns of a hundred summers.

Guards straightened as they approached, looking curiously at the blind old man and his limping companion. Both were thick with grey dust and stumbling with fatigue. The fatigue was genuine: it had been a long difficult walk for them over the plain and down the narrow road, the more so because one could barely see and the other scarcely walk.

Leon halted at the sight of levelled spears, feeling the impact as Grochen stumbled into him. He blinked reddened eyes as Grochen's quavering voice lashed at him.

'Again you halt! For this you will be beaten when we reach a place of rest. Was ever a man cursed with so stupid a guide?'

Leon turned, mouthing thick, unintelligible words, a trickle of saliva running from his mouth over his chin.

'What's that you say? A village? The Lord be praised.' Grochen jerked at the rope. 'Well, why do you wait? Enter, and find us water and shade.'

'Not so fast, old man.' The elder of the guards stepped forward and peered into the milky orbs. 'Where are you from?'

'The coast.' Grochen did not look towards the man. 'Since Spring we have travelled, seeking the shrine at Medos where I hope to be cured of my affliction. Is this place Medos?'

'This is the Node-Village Thromart in the heart of the Mesh,' said the guard. 'I've never heard of Medos.'

'Never heard of the blessed Shrine where all the ills afflicting man can be washed away?' Grochen lifted his voice. 'What ill besets me? What evil have I done to be so cursed with a fool too doltish to find his way?' Lifting the end of the rope, he lashed out at the boy, who cowered, covering his head.

'Hold!' The guard caught the rope and twitched it from Grochen's hand. 'The boy is not a beast to be beaten. Without him where would you be?' He stooped and looked into Leon's face. 'Tell me, lad. What was the name of the last village at which you stayed?' He scowled as Leon mouthed gibberish. 'What is wrong with you? Why cannot you answer?'

Grochen shuffled forward, his voice the whine of a beggar. 'My Lord, he is afflicted both in body and mind. A poor thing sent by the All-Seeing to guide my footsteps on their way. Last night we slept in a place of stone amid bushes of thorn. This morning the sun was warm against my back.'

One of the guards said, 'The messenger from Weitonburg spoke of a man and a boy. These could be the ones for whom the Provost offered the reward.'

'A blind man and an idiot boy?' The eldest guard frowned. 'Weitonburg is to the west and south but these came from the east.'

'Even so, they could be the same.' The guard slipped his dagger from its sheath. He knelt, ran his left hand up Leon's kirtle, and seized the soft bag hanging between his legs. The edge of the blade was a burning icicle as it touched the flesh.

Leon cried out, body stiff with terror, fear clogging his throat so that his protest was garbled. He caught a glimpse of watchful eyes and, just in time, recognised the action for the test it was. Spittle dribbled over his chin as he mouthed an incoherent stream of sounds.

The guard straightened, looked at the bright blade of his his dagger and then, without warning, thrust it at Grochen's face. He did not flinch until the point touched his cheek and then he stepped back, slapping at the spot of blood.

'I've been stung!' he cried. 'An insect has taken my blood!'

The eldest guard looked at his companion. 'A blind old man and an idiot boy,' he said. 'Satisfied?'

'Aye.' The man sheathed his dagger. 'They are what they seem. Let them pass.'

The walls were thick, the shadows cool, yet Leon's body was clammy with sweat. He lunged forward, halting as the noose tightened around his neck. Grochen's voice was a rumble in his ear.

'Steady, boy. The deception is not ended yet. And, if we are stopped and tested again, urinate a little. It would be normal for an idiot to piss himself with fear.'

Beyond the wall lay a maze of narrow streets flanked with houses which leaned towards each other as they rose towards the sky. They were compact dwellings, once teeming with warren-like life, now half empty as that life had moved from the Node-Village to found other, smaller villages in the Mesh. Thromart was a place of fading glories, many of the buildings showing signs of neglect, the streets uneven, the dusty gutters choked with garbage.

Only the central plaza had remained unchanged. Here stood the communal pump, the open trough of water, scummed but welcomingly cool. Leon drank, thrusting his head deep into the liquid, feeling the wetness of it on face and neck. A woman, big breasted and broad hipped, screamed a curse as he splashed her kirtle. The curse faltered as he gabbled and wet himself. The woman's tone softened as she recognised one of the Afflicted.

To Grochen she said, 'Your son, master?'

'My eyes.' He lifted a hand towards his milky orbs. 'We

travel to the Shrine at Medos. Now we need food and a place to rest. My blessing, woman, if you will direct our steps.'

'The tavern has no welcome for those who cannot pay, but Landis, at the stable, is a kindly man. For small service he will let you sleep in the straw.'

'And food?'

'That also, if you find favour in his sight.' The woman knelt. 'Your blessing, master?'

He gave it, moving his right hand in a mystical gesture, asking directions as she rose. The stable was at the far side of the village, a long, low building, heavy with the stench of manure and urine. Landis came to meet them, a squat man wearing a leather apron, his face seamed, dirt lying thick in the creases.

'Food and rest,' he said. 'Granted. A crust and a place in the straw. In return you will pump water until noon and the boy will clean up the stalls. Agreed?'

'You are kind,' said Grochen. 'Could I ask for one more thing? A bucket of water to lave away the stains of travel?'

When they were alone in a nest of malodorous straw, Grochen peeled the membranes from his eyes and plunged his face into the bucket of water, blinking furiously as he rose. His eyes were bloodshot, the edges rimmed with angry soreness. He washed again, dipping his head and scrubbing the dust from his hair, then turned to where Leon lay sprawling. Gently he touched the fevered brow.

'Bad,' he said. 'Your blood is on fire. When it is solid dark we'll find a doctor.'

Leon stirred. 'And Landis?'

'To hell with him. His charity is a fake. A solid morning's work from the two of us for a mouldy crust and a bed in rotting straw. Forget him.'

The door was an arched panel set in a wall of stone, the sign that of a knife painted red against a background of white, the doctor himself a small man with a forked beard and eyes shrewd beneath bristling eyebrows. He stooped over Leon where he lay on a table, the light from a lantern shining through thinning hair, throwing little gleams from the tufts growing from his ears. His hands were spatulate, the tips blunt, the fingers strong. About him hung a tavern odour, a reek of strong waters and vinegar.

He pursed his lips as he examined the unbandaged leg. The wounds were edged with green and brown, the flesh puffed, thin streaks of red reached towards the knee. Moving to a sink, he poured liquid from a bottle into a basin and washed his hands. The tavern reek grew stronger. Doctor Shen Tracey used brandy for other purposes than drinking. Gently he probed the limb, frowning at Leon's gasp of pain.

'When did this happen?'

'Days ago.' Grochen loomed huge against the light. 'He fell into a klarge pit and the thing clawed him before he could escape.'

'And you kept him walking?'

'Yes, doctor, there was nothing else we could do.' Grochen looked at the boy. 'Can you cure him?'

'Cure?' Tracey shrugged. 'You have left it very late, my friend, and I am not a magician. Treat him, certainly, but before I do that, there are things we should discuss. Payment, for one. You have money?'

Leon heard Grochen's low rumble, the higher pitch of the doctor as they moved to one side. He felt strangely light-headed, almost as if he were floating, and in the light cast by the lantern, things took on a weird aspect. Jars of crystal seemed to be a row of watching eyes. A cage in which something moved seemed to pulse and swell, at one moment gigantic the next minuscule. The air itself writhed as if thick with vapours and the light, subdued as it was, hurt his eyes.

He closed them and felt a sudden nausea. Hastily he opened them, with a stab of fear. Was he dying? Was this to be the end of his life?

He lifted himself on both elbows, watching as Grochen and

the doctor haggled, the big man offering the things he had stolen lauding their value, a desperate note in his deep rumble. And something more, a hint of menace which Tracey would have been a fool not to have recognised.

'All right,' he said. 'For what you offer I will treat the boy. But I can guarantee nothing. It may be that I shall have to remove his leg. This you must accept.'

Grochen sucked in his breath. 'Is it as bad as that?'

'It isn't good. He will have to stay here under my care.'

'And I?'

'You may see him often, but I cannot support two for the price of one.' The doctor bustled about his surgery, bottles clinking, liquids gurgling. 'Here, use this to lave your eyes, they are too sore to be natural. And now, my friend, inhale this.' He came to Leon's side, a pad in his hand the acrid odour stinging as it cleared the mist from his brain. 'Relax. This is not going to hurt. A simple device to remove the poison.'

From a cage he removed a broad, furred creature as large as his palm, holding it from above and setting it gently on the inflamed flesh. Leon winced as a multitude of hollow teeth sank into his skin, the pain dying at once as the thing gorged itself on his blood.

The numbness spread, climbing up his leg, his chest, detaching his mind so that he floated in a region of strange dreams. Faces came to him from a cloud of smoke Tracey's, Grochen's, that of a young girl, the seamed mask of Elder Philbart, the dirty creases of Landis. Light interspersed with darkness, flickering, unreal. Voices came, echoing as if from the end of a tube the bottom of a well.

'The infection has progressed too far. My arts are baffled. If his life is to be saved, then the leg must be removed.'

'No! There must be another way! More money?'

'Money cannot buy health, only skill. This I have given. To wait longer is to risk losing all.'

Sweat and pain and burning fires. The taste of strange

liquids, the stench of noisome odours, the swarming nightmares of delirium. And a voice, roaring, demanding.

'Leon listen to me. You're ill, sick unto death, and there's nothing anyone here can do. But your mother was a sensitive, she had the gift of healing. You are the flesh of her flesh. You must also have that gift. Use it, boy. Use it!'

His mother! She came to him, wreathed in flame, the hair burning, the skin peeling, the very flesh bubbling from her bones. His screams echoed from the building so that those in the street walked quickly away making ritual gestures for protection. But his mother did not leave. She came closer, closer, and suddenly she was no longer burning.

He felt the coolness of her hand, the touch of her hair, the warm, comforting presence of her love. He was a small child again and she was soothing his pain, washing it away, summoning power to send through her fingers into his body. His mother with her wonderful gift. The gift he too possessed. The power he too could generate and direct, from the secret recesses of his mind.

He woke and looked up at a ceiling of painted boards, the cracks filled with plaster so that the surface was a smooth, glowing white touched with drifting shadow. He felt weak but very cool, content to lie on what seemed to be a soft white cloud. One of the shadows moved, and he turned his head to stare into a face. It was one he had seen before, young, fresh, girlishly soft.

'Hello,' she said. 'I'm Lekia. My daddy is a famous doctor. He saved your life.'

Memory caused Leon to move, to feel for his legs.

'It's all right,' she gurgled, amused. 'He didn't have to take it off. He was going to, but then you started to heal all of a sudden.' She stooped and lifted a bowl of soup. 'You're very weak, and have to build up your strength, so you must be a good boy and eat this all up.' She spooned liquid into his mouth. 'We're going to be friends. You're going to stay here with us, and my daddy is going to teach you how to help him.

You've got something he can use, an . . .' she frowned, 'an asset. Your daddy told him about it.'

'Grochen? Leon reared up in the bed. 'Where is he?'

'Gone.' She was quite matter-of-fact. 'They caught him stealing and cut off his head. So you've got to stay with us because there's nowhere else you can go.' She held the spoon to his mouth. 'Now drink your soup before it gets cold.'

TWO

Lekia was a year older than Leon but, at fifteen, she was still a child. Gaily she pirouetted about the chamber, touching jars, peering into vats, teasing somnolent creatures in their wickerwork cages. Her dress, tight around her bust and full about the hips, swirled as she moved, revealing curved thighs, milky in their whiteness. She hated and avoided the sun, saying, with truth, that only the low-born were tanned and that ladies of quality were known for the whiteness of their skin.

'When we get to Artois I shall have a maidservant and lots of dresses. My own chair, even, with strong guards to escort me through the streets when I go shopping or paying visits. Oh, Leon! Won't it be wonderful!'

He sat at a table at one end of the chamber, a sombre place filled with the appurtenances of the doctor's trade. The air was heavy with the scent of the raw materials he used for lotions, ointments, pills, poultices and salves. Light came through high-set louvres, glimmers of sunlight touching dried specimens, shining from the bleached bones of a complete human skeleton, bright against piled chiton, dull against heaps of withered fungi. Apparatus stood on long benches, retorts, alembics, constructions of stone and crystal. Ignoring the babble of the girl Leon concentrated on the mixture he was pounding in a thick, stone mortar.

'Leon!' She was impatient to talk of the good times ahead.

'Why do you always have to be so busy? Aren't you excited at the thought of leaving Thromart for a real town?'

'Your father needs this preparation,' he said, not looking up from his work. 'But I can listen while you talk.'

The years had fleshed his bones and increased his stature, and hard work had developed the muscles beneath his skin. Tracey was a hard taskmaster. Doting on his motherless daughter, he had seen no reason to be gentle with the new addition to his household. Leon had more than earned every scrap of food and instruction.

Weighing out a portion of dried insects, he added them to the mixture within the mortar and crushed them beneath the pestle. 'When do we leave?'

'Soon.' Anticipation caused her to pirouette again about the chamber. 'As soon as daddy has sold the practice. He's negotiating now with a buyer from Shenville and, as soon as the contract is signed, we'll be on our way. Think of it, Leon! A big house with servants, and the finest of foods. Nobles, perhaps, coming to dine, and fine ladies visiting at all hours. Parties and balls and entertainers. We'll be rich and respected.

'Your father is that now.'

'In Thromart yes, but the world is bigger than the Mesh, Leon. On the coast are great cities each holding more people than all the villages put together. In such a place his skill will receive its just reward.'

'And you?' He looked up from the mortar. 'What do you hope to gain?'

'I told you. A servant, guards, fine clothes, all the things a girl dreams of.'

'And a husband?' His blue eyes were very direct. 'A rich, young lord, perhaps, to give you position and title?'

She stood before him, her eyes searching his face. Was he jealous? It was impossible to tell. The smooth features framed by the thick mane of hair were as impassive as always. She had never seen him cry and rarely did he smile. Only once had he acted like the other boys of her acquaintance, and that had been one evening when, inflamed by the demands of puberty, he had reached for her, his hands questing over her flesh.

Almost she had yielded, would have yielded but for the sudden return of her father, and since then instinct and caution had restrained her ardour. Her virginity was too precious to throw away on a landless boy, no matter how handsome he might be. But perhaps later, after she was safely married?

She wrinkled her nose as he poured a few drops of oily liquid into the mortar and turned the powdered ingredients into a paste. 'What's that for?'

'Boils, contusions and eruptions of the skin,' he said drily. 'It is also a salve for aches and inner pains.' He scooped up the mess and filled a small pottery jar, sealing the lid with a touch of wax. 'Your father needs it for the captain of the Provost's guard.'

'Beeshan?' she frowned. 'Will it cure him?'

'He will be cured.' Leon rose, washed his hands then laved them with spirit. 'You'd best get upstairs. The surgery is full and there will be no time for chatter.'

'There never is,' she said acidly. 'Daddy keeps me locked away like a precious gem and you are always too busy to be fun. The sooner we get to Artois the better I shall like it. I'm fed up with this stinking village!'

She flounced from the chamber to climb the stairs and to spend the next few hours dressing her hair or sorting out the things she would take on the journey. That, or to dull the ears of the old woman who cooked and tended the house, with her incessant babble. Leon watched her go, catching a glimpse of tender thighs, the profile of her breasts. Then, picking up the jar, he went to join his master.

Tracey was in the inner surgery, a patient lying on the table, another sitting in the chair. Beeshan, on the table was a thick-set burly man of late middle-age. His pants were lowered and his tunic pulled high to reveal the hairy swell of his belly. He grunted as the doctor probed.

'Careful! That hurts like a spear!'

'It won't hurt for long.' Tracey took the jar from Leon's hand. 'This salve will cure you. Apply it thickly night and morning, rubbing it well in and covering it with clean cloth. Drink no wine or spirits, eat neither meat nor bread and go with no women for the next ten days.' Casually he turned to Leon. 'This case is of interest,' he said. 'Feel to the right of the stomach close to the groin. You have no objection, Captain?'

Leon gave the man no chance to object. He rested his hands on the swollen belly, resting the tips of his fingers where he felt an inner hardness and heat. Tissues were swollen, inflamed, angry as they gathered poison. He concentrated on the generation of his power, the ability he had inherited from his mother, sending it from his mind into the body beneath his hands.

'A bad case master,' he said, looking at the doctor. 'It is fortunate that you caught it in time.'

'Bad?' Beeshan reared from the table. 'How bad?'

'It is a severe contusion of the inner membranes,' said Tracey smoothly. 'Had you neglected it another day I would have had to cut. As it is, my salve will effect a cure – providing you do exactly as I say. Remember now: no wine, meat, bread or women for ten days. Spend the next three in bed and use the salve as directed.'

As the captain left the doctor gestured to the man in the chair. 'This one is for you, Leon. A simple cataract. Tend him while I eat.'

The man was a farmer from one of the Mesh villages, his clothing poor, his skin burned by the sun. A man with little money and no position. The pupils of both eyes were clouded by cataracts, the milky orbs reminding Leon forcibly of Grochen.

'Can you help me, master?' The man's voice held a desperate pleading. 'I gave the doctor all the money I had. I've walked for twenty days to get here. Can you help me?'

'I will help you,' said Leon.

'You?' The man frowned. 'You sound a mere boy – how can a boy help? I need a doctor, a man of skill and experience. I've paid. I sold my farm and all I owned. I've paid, I tell you!'

Paid, but not enough for Tracey to concern himself. Fame had made him arrogant and ambition had fed his greed. Leon's gift had wrought amazing cures but always the credit went to the doctor's potions and salves.

Quietly he soothed the man. 'I am skilled. I promise that you will see again. Now relax, look upwards, hold your head still.'

First he washed the eye with a dilute extract of insect venom to numb the muscles and rob the nerves of feeling. From a container of seething water he lifted a wooden handle set with a slender shaft of pointed steel. Carefully he inserted the needle beneath the outer membrane of the right eye and then, with methodical care, squeezed the opaque mass of aqueous tissue away from the pupil and through the opening.

The man sucked in his breath. 'I can see! Thank God, I can see!'

The left eye followed. Leon dropped the needle back into the seething water, again washed the eyes with a weak dilution of cleansing elements, and rested the tips of his fingers gently beside both eyes.

'You must avoid bright lights and glare. It would be best for you to spend the next four days in a darkened room. If you must travel, then wear a bandage over your eyes. I will give you a lotion. Wash both eyes night, morning and noon. Use fresh liquid each time and for each eye. You understand?

Tracey joined him as the man left. He brushed crumbs from his coat, gems winking on his spatulate hands, more gems glowing from his tufted ears. 'You operated successfully?'

'Yes, doctor. He will see again.'

'Unless infection sets in and makes both eyes permanently

blind.' Tracey was cynical. 'Well, no matter, his fee was too small for us to care.'

'It was all he had,' said Leon quietly. 'And there will be no infection.'

'Your power?' The doctor frowned. 'You waste it on such people. I have warned you before; it must be reserved for those whom I decide should benefit. You gave him a lotion?'

'Yes.'

'That, at least, you remembered. Now get my bag. We are needed at the Provost's.'

Leon heard the sound of retching as they climbed the stairs. The Provost's house was the third largest in Thromart; surpassed only by that of the Mayor's, and the meeting hall itself. But even in the Node-Village, no house was really grand, and the plastered walls caught and reflected the sound. Servants, bondsmen mostly, scurried about like a pack of frightened dogs, carrying basins, jugs of mulled wine and stone bottles of hot water. From an upper room the Provost's strong voice rose above the babble.

'Has the doctor arrived? Send men to search the town. Hurry, or I'll flay your hides!'

Tracey slowed his feet. 'It seems that Provost Malkin is in good health,' he mused. 'Who then, is in need of aid?'

It was the guest of the Provost's, a broad, sun-burned man with grizzled hair and a scarred cheek. He lay sprawled on a bed, his embroidered tunic stained with vomit, his face contorted with pain.

'Kell Piriton,' said the Provost. 'An envoy from His Grace the Duke Morford. We were at dinner when he collapsed. I had him carried upstairs and sent for you immediately.'

Tracey looked at the sick man. 'He collapsed, you say?'

'As if he had been speared. He was drinking wine and showered it over the company. Then he clutched at his belly and fell, spewing his food.' The Provost's fingers tugged at his curled beard. 'Poison?'

'Perhaps.' The doctor stepped forward and sniffed at the stained tunic. 'Was anyone else affected?'

'No.'

'And all ate the same food? Drank the same wine?'

'Yes.'

'Then the likelihood of poison is small. It could, no doubt, have been slipped into his goblet by a servitor, but who would want to wish him dead in Thromart?' Tracey sniffed again. 'Did he complain of any pain at all? Prior to his collapsing?'

'No. He was stiff from his ride, of course, and asked for a warm bath.'

'Age would account for the stiffness,' said the doctor. 'We could question his attendants but I doubt if it would help. Boy! Remove his clothing.'

With a sharp knife Leon cut away the stained tunic, the pants which hugged the thick thighs, the mesh underwear beneath. On the gross belly stood a nodule dark with congestion. Tracey drew in his breath.

'A strangulated hernia,' he said. 'It must be relieved at once. Have servants bring me hot water and clean towels. Quickly!'

With steaming cloths he tried to relax the taut muscle clamping the trapped intestine. Piriton shrieked his agony as he tried more ruthlessly direct methods. Sweating the doctor looked at his assistant.

'Get a rope,' he snapped. 'Find a strong man and a beam. Hurry!'

Servants carried the patient to where a great hook hung from an overhead beam. Tracey threw the rope over it, lashed it to the sick man's ankles and snapped orders at the stalwart guard.

'Pull! Raise him!'

The weight was too great. The guard grunted as he felt the muscles in back and shoulders yield beneath the strain. Hoarsely he summoned a companion and together they hauled the dead weight off the floor. Hanging head-down, swinging a little, the envoy of the Duke hung like a slaughtered beast.

'We must thrust the protruding intestine back into the stomach and close the muscle-wall behind it,' said Tracey. 'I could operate but if we can relieve the situation a truss will serve.' He watched the swinging figure. 'Soon he will be unconscious and the muscles will relax due to his unnatural position. Prepare me more hot towels.'

Again he set to work, grunting with satisfaction as the nodule disappeared beneath his hands.

'Lower him now. Gently.'

A knotted towel and a broad leather belt served as an emergency truss. Acrid odours filled the chamber as he restored the envoy's senses. Piriton blinked, gagged, looked surprised when he did not retch.

'Rest easy, my lord,' said the doctor. 'I have cured your condition. Soon all pain will have ceased.' He glanced at a servant. 'Bring a cup of wine, warmed to blood heat, flavoured with honey.' To the brew he added five drops from a vial. 'Drink this, my lord.'

Piriton blew out his cheeks as he handed back the empty cup. 'That was bad,' he said. 'It was like a spear twisting in my guts. I owe you much for what you have done.'

'Your life, my lord,' said the doctor blandly. 'Without my skill you would have died. Sleep now. When you wake I shall attend you.'

The Provost waited at the foot of the stairs. He grunted with relief when he heard the news, and threw an arm about Tracey's shoulders. 'You did well. It would have been a bad thing for the Duke's envoy to have died in my house. Come, let us drink to your success.'

Leon followed them into a side chamber, unnoticed or ignored. He was tired, ravenous and hunched down in the shadows as the others talked.

'There is trouble on the edges of the Mesh. A band of brigands is ravaging the villages. The Duke has decided to summon a levy. Each village must provide men and horses to form a troop against the enemy. They must be found and destroyed.'

'That will not be easy,' said the doctor quietly. 'And it may take a long time.'

'Too long.' The Provost poured more wine. 'And the thing can't be done cheaply. The men and horses have to be fed and supplied. A tax will have to be made on all according to their wealth.'

Tracey sipped thoughtfully at his wine. 'Has the proclamation been made yet?'

'No. We were discussing terms when he collapsed.'

'And these brigands – where are they operating?'

'To the south and east.' The Provost shrugged as he reached again for the wine jug. 'They could be mercenaries from the coast trying to pick up some easy loot before heading back to sea. Personally I think they are, but the Duke wants to take no chances. The Mesh is a poor place, but even so it is under his protection. But it will not be easy to raise the taxes. Not one crop in three is really good and one in five fails.' He slammed his hand on the table. 'And what have we to use for men? Farmers unused to the saddle. Traders and merchants who would be rubbed raw in a day. A pity your arts can't devise something to keep such men from pain.'

'They can and I have.' Tracey covered his goblet, shaking his head as the Provost hefted the jug. 'Boy!'

Leon rose and stepped towards the table.

'Bare your arm.' The doctor picked a knife from the table, an eating implement of polished silver, dull but with a point. Deliberately he pressed the point against the naked flesh.

'You see? He does not flinch.' He shifted the point and pressed again. 'The boy was infected by klarge venom when he was young. I cured him, but there was an interesting development. The klarge poison numbs sensitivity so that the victim remains conscious to the end. It does not destroy the sensation of pain but lessens it so that a minor injury can be ignored. This venom could be prepared, diluted and given to your levies.'

'You will do this?'

Tracey shook his head. 'Not I,' he said quietly. 'But the one who is buying my practice. I will leave notes so that he knows what is to be done. Of course, should he learn of the brigands and the proposed taxes he might not be interested in buying it and so –'

'He will not learn,' interrupted the Provost. 'I shall see to it in return for some slight token of your appreciation. I shall do more. The envoy is taking the road to Artois and can hardly refuse to escort you after what you have done. When will he be ready to travel?'

'In three days. If he uses a litter, one.'

'He will use a litter,' said the Provost. He poured more wine and this time Tracey made no effort to prevent him filling both goblets. 'To a happy journey.'

They drank.

The column was a crippled snake winding along the road in the heat of the mid-summer sun. A dozen horsemen sweated in their mail, glancing enviously at the litters in one of which the envoy lounged, the other being shared by the doctor and his daughter. Mostly Tracey rode, sitting awkwardly in the saddle, trying, Leon guessed, to master a social art while he still had the time and opportunity. Lekia didn't care. Ladies did not ride and she had no intention of learning. Leon wasn't give the chance. He drove the cart piled high with the doctor's goods, the sealed chests containing his wealth, the bales of medicines and books.

A horseman riding alongside the vehicle hawked and spat. 'Boy,' he said, 'would there be a flask of wine in that load?'

'Yes,' said Leon. 'But it's the doctor's private supply.'

'To be shared with the envoy, no doubt.' The man scowled, beads of sweat running from beneath the rim of his helmet, tracing paths through the dust which greyed his features. 'All we get is the swill served up in the villages and tonight we won't even get that. It'll be hard bread and sour water and not much of either.' He turned in his saddle, looking back over the column, the pack horses plodding beneath their loads. 'If you could manage to get me a drink of that wine I'll teach you how to hold a sword.'

'I know how to hold a sword.'

'You? A doctor's assistant?' The man laughed. 'A sword isn't a knife and you won't be using it against someone who can't hit back.'

Leon didn't bother to argue. He had learned the basic military arts in the gymnasium at Thromart where a scarred veteran earned his keep by teaching the sons of traders and merchants. Leon had paid in kind, using his knowledge and pilfered ointments to bandage cuts and bruises. He had learned other things too, among them a realisation of his own ignorance.

The world wasn't just a collection of farming villages, nor was it a string of towns along the coast. There were other places, other worlds and one day, perhaps, he would see them.

'That's a plump, white pigeon we've got with us.' The horseman was hot and bored and eager to break the monotony of the journey. He winked as he nodded towards the litter in which Lekia rode. 'Soft, juicy, tender meat. I bet you've handled it a time or two, eh?'

Leon slapped the reins against the flank of the horse.

'Don't want to talk about it? Well, I understand. But if I was your age, and lived in the same house she did, I'd do a lot of walking at night. You know, slip between the sheets while she was asleep and give her something to dream about. From the look of her she wouldn't object too strongly. Not if you knew what you were doing. I could tell you just how to go about it if you'd get me a drink of that wine.'

Something flashed on the horizon. Leon stood up, looking towards it, shading his eyes.

'Something wrong?'

'A brightness on the skyline. It's gone now.'

'Probably the sun on a rock,' said the guard casually. 'How about it, boy? Get me some wine and I'll teach you how to make a woman scream with delight.'

'I can't,' said Leon shortly. 'It isn't mine. If you want some ask the doctor. Here he comes now.'

Tracey reined alongside the cart, dismounted, tied the animal to the tailboard and climbed up to sit beside Leon. He glared at the horseman, who spurred his mount and rode a little ahead.

'What was that man talking about?'

'The load,' said Tracey. 'He wanted some wine.'

'Is that all?' Tracey was worried about his treasures. He glanced at the boxes containing them, reassuring himself that all was safe. The journey was taking longer than he had anticipated. The envoy had insisted on taking a wide swing to outlying villages and now they would have to camp in the open. 'How did he know we carried wine?'

'I told him.' Leon didn't look at the man at his side. 'I didn't know it was a secret.'

'You should have held your tongue. These men are scum, for all that they work for the Duke. If they knew what we carried they would cut our throats and steal it all.'

The doctor's concern was clouding his judgement; the men were rough but would remain loyal. A bloated fly settled on the flank of the horse. Leon flipped the reins, crushing it, watching as it fell to the dust. He said, 'I must speak with you, doctor.'

'About what?'

'About me, my life, the future. What will happen when we reach Artois?'

'Happen?' Tracey looked sharply at the boy. 'I have bought a house and will commence to build a new practice. I shall accept students and sell potions. What else did you expect?'

'Nothing, but what will my position be?'

'What it is now. You will work with me, learning and helping, doing what you can. Later, if you behave yourself, I might accept you as a student without fee. In time you could even become a doctor yourself.' He sensed Leon's disappointment. 'Isn't that good enough? I took you in, provided you with a home, fed you, supplied your clothes, taught you valuable knowledge. What else do you expect?'

'Money,' said Leon. 'A wage at least. I help you a lot and there are things I'd like to buy. I don't want to be a bondservant all my life.'

He heard the sharp hiss of indrawn breath, saw the glitter of gems on the spatulate hands. The blow, when it fell, was not unexpected.

'You ingrate! Have I ever said that you were a servant? I saved your life, remember. Think of that when you brood on fancied wrongs.'

Leon lifted his hand, touched his cheek, looked at the stain of blood on his flesh. 'And you think of my talent,' he said quietly. 'The cures for which you get the credit. From now on you had better rely on your own skill.'

He expected another blow but it didn't come. For a while they rode in silence and then the doctor said, 'You are young, but not too young to understand what I am going to say. Your mother was burned as a witch. The man who brought you to me was a wanted criminal. I should have turned you both over to the Provost; instead I took care of you when you were left alone. It was a risk I was then willing to take, but perhaps now the risk is too great. Continue to defy me and I shall have to send you back to Weitonburg.'

He rose and jumped from the cart, untying his horse and clumsily mounting.

'Remember,' he said, riding close. 'Villagers have long memories.'

They camped that night in a shallow bowl filled with stunted shrub and indifferent grass. Smoke from the camp fires rose slender and straight in the still air, tracing thin pillars of darkness against the spangled sky. To one side the horses browsed, restless, the thud of their hooves mingling with the champ of their jaws. There was no spring, each man watering his horse from the skin he carried. The tent of the envoy glowed with inner light, shadows crossing the fabric as the doctor tended to his patient. At a discreet distance his own tent, which he would share with Lekia, stood dark, the flap open. Behind it stood the cart with Leon on guard.

He rose as something rustled close, sinking back as he saw the pale glimmer of a face, the soft shine of fabric.

'Leon?' She climbed into the cart and sat beside him as he lay, his face towards the sky. 'Leon? Are you asleep?'

'No.'

'What are you doing then? Thinking?'

'Yes.'

'About Artois?'

'About a lot of things.' He pointed towards the stars. 'Look at them. They make patterns in the sky and men guide themselves by them across land and sea. Just as if they were beacons. But they are more than that. Each one is a sun just like our own and each one has worlds just like this. No,' he corrected himself, 'not just like this. Different. New animals and plants and colours in the sky. Did you know that?'

'Of course I know it. I've been to school. But what difference does it make? This is our world and we must make the best of it. When we get to Artois I'm going to learn how to act like a lady. A real lady, I mean, someone like the envoy's daughter. When daddy gets famous I'll have to run the house and arrange banquets and things. Oh, Leon! I can hardly wait!'

He looked at her face in the starlight, bright and radiant with anticipation. She, at least, felt no dissatisfaction, but then she had a future. Something on which to plan and build. A stairway to contentment if not to happiness. Would he feel different if he had the same?

A brilliant streak crossed the sky, fading as it fell to die just above the horizon. Lekia squealed as she saw it.

'Leon! Quickly! Make a wish!'

'I've made it.'

'Tell me what it was.'

'I wish I could travel,' he said slowly. 'To see all the things that are waiting to be seen. To learn and to get somewhere. To have men obey me, perhaps.'

'To become a Lord? But, Leon, you can't! You're going to live with us. You know that.'

'Perhaps your father has other ideas,' he said drily. He touched his cheek where a ring had torn his flesh. 'We quarrelled today. I asked him to pay me a wage and he hit me.'

'You shouldn't have upset him, Leon. Daddy is good and kind and tries to do the best for us all. And why do you want money? He gives you everything you need. You shouldn't be greedy.'

Like father like daughter, he thought, but that wasn't wholly true. He would never have lifted his arms to embrace the doctor. Lekia stiffened at his touch and then relaxed, snuggling against him as he pressed his hand against the soft mound of her breasts, letting it drop to the smooth curve of her thighs.

'Leon!' she whispered. 'Don't!'

The hem of her dress lifted and starlight shone on milky skin.

'No!' Her breath came faster against his cheek. 'You mustn't!'

'Why not?' There was a fire in his blood, the demanding flame of youth, and she was warm and smooth and close against him. 'No one need ever know.'

But she would know, and her husband-to-be would know, and the thought quelled her passion. To caress and touch and to feel his desire was one thing, to allow him to have his way with her was another. As his fingers began to probe she writhed from his arms.

'No! Don't do that! Touch me again and I'll scream!'

A child with the body of a woman, younger now than she

had ever been, cherished, spoiled, using him for her selfish pleasure. As her father used him to build his fame and fortune. And, in return, both gave the same reward.

Nothing.

She saw the anger in his face, the cold eyes and the mouth suddenly cruel, and backed against the bales in the body of the cart.

'Leon! Don't look at me like that! Leon!'

Her cry was echoed from the edge of the camp. It was repeated close to hand and a guard came stumbling from the scrub, slamming against the side of the cart and falling, a dark gush of blood pulsing from his severed throat. At once everything was pandemonium. A bull-voice rose above the shouts and cries.

'To arms! We are attacked!'

They came, limned in the starlight, a score of them with faces like wolves, rising from the scrub through which they had crept. The guards who should have watched but who had dozed, confident in their safety, were the first to die. The rest quickly followed.

Leon jumped from the cart to where the man had fallen, and snatched up his sword. It was heavy, a length of edged and pointed metal without true balance, a tool needing brute strength to wield. He lifted it as a shape came running towards him, trying to remember his lessons, throwing up the blade as starlight splintered from steel lashing towards his head.

In theory he should have caught the opposing sword, deflecting it while his own blade circled to thrust at the snarling face beneath the pointed helmet. In fact he only managed to prevent the edge from biting into his skull, turning the blade so that the flat smashed against his temple.

As he fell he heard Lekia scream.

There was a buzzing in his ears, a fat, sleepy sound which heightened in pitch as he moved. A cloud of flies rose from his temple, circling, metallic greenish bodies bright in the light of late morning. They buzzed away as he flapped his hand, settling elsewhere as he rose. The ground moved beneath his feet and he fell on all fours, retching with a sudden nausea, hammers pounding at the soft surface of his brain. After a long while he moved again, catching the side of the cart to support himself while he examined his wound.

The side of his face was stiff with dried blood, more of it matting his hair on the right side, and he sucked in his breath as his questing fingers found a swollen lump crossed by an open gash. The blow had broken the skin but had not shattered the bone beneath. In that, at least, he had been lucky.

Thirst was a raging torment. He searched the body of the cart. The boxes were gone, the bales slit open and their contents strewn all around. Turning, he stumbled to where the tent of the envoy rested, now a collapsed mass of silk. He stooped and pulled it away from what lay beneath. Piriton looked at him with dead eyes. His belly had been ripped open, blood and intestines a noisome mess, the whole covered with a crawling mass of feeding flies.

He jerked free of the tent and found a skin of water, almost empty and disdained by the men who had attacked. He drank, and poured the remainder over his his head, the wetness easing his pain. Only then did he look around.

The camp was a shambles. Men sprawled in various attitudes of death, a few strangers, the rest wearing the livery of the Duke. Most had been stripped of weapons and armour, all had been robbed of rings, chains and items of value. He looked at one of the strangers. The man's face was dark, the lips full, a thin black moustache gracing the upper lip. The eyes were savage, slanting in a manner he had never seen before, the hair black and curled tightly against the skull.

They must have watched the little column all through the hot day, riding below the horizon except when checking the progress of the envoy. The flash he had seen could only have come from the sunlight reflecting from a weapon, too far off and too brief to have been spotted by others. At night they had moved quietly towards the fires, killing the guards and then coming in with a rush. He was alive only because he had fallen beneath a blow, the shadows and the blood giving the appearance of death.

He remembered hearing Lekia scream and turned towards the cart. She was nowhere to be seen. The doctor's tent lay flat and he tugged at the fabric. Tracey lay below, the lobes of his ears bloody where gems had been ripped away, his thick fingers severed for the sake of his rings. A knife had ripped his throat so that he seemed to be laughing as he looked at the sky, the red orifice of his gaping mouth topped by the stained mat of his beard.

He found the girl on the other side of the camp.

She had been stripped, and lay straddled on the ground, blood and moisture thick between the rounded thighs, the soft, white flesh marred with ugly bruises. Thongs held wrists and ankles to stakes driven in the soil and her body showed marks of torment. The knife which had slipped into her heart must have brought a merciful release.

Rising, Leon searched the hollow with his eyes. The horses had gone, the pack animals with their loads. The raiders must have waited until dawn, eating, drinking, amusing themselves, until there was light enough to make a clean sweep of the dead. And then they had headed to the south and east, rich with unexpected plunder, eager to get back to the coast and safety.

Slowly he moved over the camp, pausing to inspect the dead, looking for water, for food, for anything of value. He was on foot, alone in the wilderness, completely lost but knowing that if he hoped to survive he had to find the means of doing so. He found a dagger, a few coins of little value, a half-skin of water and some stale bread. The cart provided a few surgical instruments and some vials of valuable drugs.

Wrapping everything into a bundle he headed towards the north.

THREE

It was a story which Charisse Dee Bouchet was never too weary to relate. Of how, while on vacation, she and her husband had rescued a boy from death.

'It was the most incredible thing. There he was, all alone, simply miles and miles from anywhere. He had no water and no food and was desperately ill. A young boy completely lost in the wilderness. It was a miracle he had managed to stay alive.'

Her listeners edged a little closer. One of them, Cyd Dee Thurston, touched the rim of hair circling his mouth. 'And this was on Rhome?'

'Yes, a terrible planet, unbelievably primitive. It has a weird ecology with lots of fantastic insects, and Rolfe wanted to collect a few. For the trophy room, he said, though I think he really wanted to prove to Manager Jay Mysie that he was just as good with a gun as Mysie could ever be. Men are such boys when it comes to things like that.'

Charisse gestured a robot to attend to the needs of her guests. Automatically she glanced beyond the circle at those around her. The big room was filled with light and colour, bubbles of scented air drifting at random, the music subdued so as not to interfere with conversation. Later it would grow louder and there would be dancing and entertainment. The party, like all her parties, was going well.

'It was rather fun in a way,' she continued. 'We had to pretend that we were a Lord and his Lady from beyond the sea and had to wear the most barbaric clothing. Of course we had protective undergarments and were loaded with prophylactics. But the food! Completely unprocessed and horribly dirty. We carried our own rations naturally, and we had a guide from the tourist agency who attended to transportation and everything. Well, there we were in camp and this boy came stumbling towards us. The guide wanted to kill him, but of course I wouldn't permit that.'

'It's a wonder he didn't insist,' said a plump woman from the edge of the circle. Privately she wondered whether, if the boy had been ugly or crippled, he would have received such consideration.

'He tried,' admitted Charisse. 'But, after all, Rolfe is a Manager and does carry some influence. We came to an arrangement; we could look after the boy providing we took him with us.'

'So you took him in and cured him and brought him back home,' said Thurston. 'An ignorant savage from a backward world.'

Charisse was quick to defend her protege. 'He is not ignorant and is not a savage. He was uneducated, true, but we took care of that with hypnotutes. Now he is as knowledgeable as anyone of his age.'

The plump woman said shrewdly, 'And physically?'

'Leon had an unpleasant childhood,' said Charisse. 'It forced him to mature very quickly. He was earning his living at an age when our children are still at school.' She smiled as she looked towards the far end of the room. 'Here he comes now, so you can judge for yourself.'

At eighteen Leon had reached his full height. The years would thicken his body and develop his muscles, but now he was all litheness and grace, taller than any present, coloured lights gleaming from hair cut short in the prevailing fashion.

He looked, thought the plump woman, like a tiger among swine, hard and firm with barbaric assurance, and she felt a sudden envy as she looked at her hostess. To have such a man owing a debt of gratitude! To have found so masculine a treasure!

'My lady!' He lifted Charisse's hand, touched it to his lips, lowered it as he straightened at her side. 'If I am late, I apologise. I was detained.'

'At the gymnasium?'

'Yes. Harden was showing me some tricks of unarmed combat and there was a thing I wished to master.'

'You fight?' Cyd Dee Thurston met the deep-set eyes. 'Barbaric games to remind you of your childhood?'

Leon smiled. 'Hardly that.'

'But you fight,' insisted Thurston. 'I too am interested in the use of primitive weapons. Perhaps we could indulge in a bout together.'

'Thurston has recently arrived from Elgar,' explained Charisse. 'He was taking care of the Family interests there. A factory and mine, wasn't it, Thurston?'

'Three factories,' he corrected. 'A mine and three thousand square miles of farmland. You were fortunate,' he said to Leon. 'You managed to attract the notice of a wealthy family. One rich enough to afford to pander to a whim.' He extended his arm to Charisse as the music swelled. 'Shall we dance?'

A tall girl with hair streaked with silver and jet came to Leon as he stood alone. Her arms were long, slender, wreathed in coils of crimson and emerald. Her gown was low at the neck, tight at the hips, the skirt slit to reveal the smooth taper of her thigh. 'You will dance with me? Please?'

She was a party-girl hired for the occasion, trained in the arts of conversation, dance, music and love. The scent of her perfume filled his nostrils as they moved in time to the mathematical beat of the music, feet treading a complex pattern on the polished floor. The music changed, developed a rhythmic pulse, woke primitive responses so that the dancers moved closer, swaying in mounting abandon.

Leon felt the yielding pressure of her breasts, the allure of her hips, the naked invitation of her throat.

'Make love to me' she whispered. 'Take me and use me. I'm so tired of these civilised fools who expect to receive more than they can give.'

He looked into her eyes. 'And I'm not civilised?'

'You're different. There's something of the animal in you.'

Her hands climbed up his back, reached his neck, dug nails into his flesh. 'I want to release it. Now!'

'You're bored,' he said. 'You should change your occupation.'

'Is that what you think?' The music changed, hard, crystalline notes blasting signals to which the dancers responded with short, robotic steps, bodies apart, arms gyrating. 'What shall I become? A housewife, perhaps? Would you marry me?'

A balloon came drifting forward and she struck at it, the scent of roses filling the air, clashing with her own perfume. Another yielded a puff of euphoric gas. Giggling she swayed close.

'I'm sorry. That was a stupid thing to say. You're riding high and don't want to throw yourself away. Charisse wouldn't like it.'

His hand caught her arm, fingers digging into the flesh. 'Meaning?'

'Nothing.' She pulled at her arm. 'Don't! You're hurting me!'

'Isn't that what you wanted?' His eyes were hard, unsmiling. 'To release the animal? Isn't that why you said what you did?'

He turned, leaving her, not waiting for an answer. A robot opened a door as he approached and he stepped out onto a high balcony. Below sprawled the vast complex of the city. On each side, lights stretched towards the horizon and the air pulsed with the activity which, on Joslen, never ceased. Tilting his head, he looked at the sky. The stars were different to those he remembered, assembled in strange configurations, blotched by the glow of racing moons. Among them rode the coloured lights of high-flying craft, the blue spears of vessels climbing into space.

'Leon?' She had followed him onto the balcony. 'Leon?'

He turned as she approached, silver and jet and milky

white, flecks of crimson and emerald sparkling from arms and the narrow belt about her waist.

'I'm sorry for what I said in there. I must have been crazy, but sometimes it gets to you. All the stupidity of it. The meaningless noise. The empty chatter, the dancing and drinking and ritual passion. And I'm getting older all the time.'

He looked at the starlight reflected in her eyes. 'I understand.'

'Do you? You should. In a way you're like me, a pet. Something to amuse them for a while. When they get tired of their toy, what then?'

'I don't know,' he said slowly. 'I've thought about it.'

'You'll be all right,' she said. 'They'll adopt you, or make you a junior executive, or something. But please, if you complain they won't book me again. I'll be blacklisted and downgraded. I'll lose all chance of finding a rich protector.'

'Don't worry,' he said. 'I won't complain.'

Rolfe Dee Bouchet said, 'Really, cousin, I fail to see how Leon can be of any concern to anyone other than myself.'

'And Charisse?'

'And my wife, naturally.'

'And the Family?'

'They are not involved.'

'Rolfe, you are so very wrong.' Cyd Dee Thurston leaned back in his contour chair and shook his head as he stared at his host. They were in the trophy room where exotic creatures stared from the walls in immobile fury; a klarge, a spinarett, an octopod from Strygia, a dozen other specimens from as many worlds. 'This is a Family matter as you must surely be aware. Do you intend to adopt the boy?'

Rolfe hesitated. 'I had considered it.'

'So Lyle suspected. He visited me on Elgar and was most concerned. I promised to adjudicate the matter.' He lifted a hand to still the other's protest. 'No, Rolfe, it has been decided, and I have been given full authority. No one blames you for having taken pity on the boy. It was most unwise of you to bring him back with you, but understandable. Now he is no longer a boy, and his future must be decided.'

'By me,' said Rolfe.

'By the Family,' corrected Thurston. 'You can defy them, of course, but you know what the consequences will be. Your income will be diminished to a basic holding which will be cancelled on your death. If you adopt the boy without permission he will not inherit. If you should die before Charisse she will be left without support. She could divorce you, of course, but knowing her she would be reluctant to do that. So what have you to gain?' He answered his own question. 'Nothing.' The strength and wealth of the Family rests on the willingness of each member to adhere to the whole.'

'I don't need the Family. I can survive without it.'

'You could survive, yes,' admitted Thurston. 'But would you be happy? I doubt it. You cannot ignore the conditioning of a lifetime and the traditions of three hundred years. You would end by hating the boy, and so what is there to gain?' He smiled, relaxing as he broke a capsule and inhaled the rising aroma. 'We aren't quarrelling, Rolfe. There is no need for that. All we need to do is to come to some understanding. As intelligent people that shouldn't be too difficult.'

Rolfe climbed to his feet and wandered restlessly about the room, pausing to look at cased weapons, a collection of gaudy-winged flies, the savage mandibles of a purple-armoured arachnid. 'What have you against Leon? He is a perfect speciman of manhood.'

'Like the trophies on your walls?' Thurston was sharp. 'Is that his appeal? You know,' he continued as Rolfe, not answering, resumed his seat, 'I listened to Charisse tell the story of how you found him, but I feel that she omitted certain details. For example it could not have been a matter of kill him or bring him back home. There must have been an alternative.'

'There was,' admitted Rolfe. 'We could have cured him and

taken him to a village. I wanted to do that, but Charisse –' He shrugged. 'I make no excuses because I am as much to blame. But if you had seen him, lying there, so young and helpless – well, I couldn't refuse her.'

'No,' said Thurston gently. 'And neither could any man who is as much in love with his wife as you are with her. A pity that she could not have had a child of her own. A greater pity that you did not agree to using your sperm for an ectogene birth.'

'I did.' Rolfe was curt. 'I too, am infertile.'

'So? I must have missed it in the records. Well, no matter, but it does explain the incident. The thing now is to resolve it to everyone's satisfaction.' Thurston broke another capsule, inhaled, and then added, quietly, 'There can however, be no possibility of the boy being adopted into the Family.'

Rolfe made no comment.

'He is totally incompatible,' explained Thurston. 'I have examined his psych-records and he would never fit in. He is a barbarian, conditioned by his early life and environment: of that there can be no doubt at all. To give him a position of responsibility and trust would be to court disaster. He would grow restless, crave action, and risk upsetting the established order for his own gratification. He would become bored with routine. He would be unable to work with other members of the Family, and would create discord. I'm sorry, Rolfe, but these things are true.'

'I'll admit that he comes from a barbaric culture,' said Rolfe slowly. 'I'll also admit that his nature must have been conditioned by the need to survive. But he has been educated. Your objections are no longer valid.'

'He has been taught certain tricks of civilisation,' corrected Thurston patiently. He had no desire to annoy or upset his elder relative. The keyword of the Family was Harmony. Only if all else failed would he use the pressure of his authority. 'And he has been taught certain facts. But this has not changed, and could not change, his basic nature. He is a barbarian, with all that that implies. He is a member of a culture totally divorced from our own. The psych-records leave the matter in no doubt – and you have other evidence. His penchant for combat-sports, for example. What other man of his age and position indulges in such pastimes? I have spoken to Hardin and he tells me that Leon fights with a savage ruthlessness which, at times, is frightening.'

'He is young,' said Rolfe. 'Four years is not a long time in which to change a nature.'

Thurston was emphatic. 'It will never change. I know. On Elgar I have had experience with barbarians. They live in the hills and spend their lives fighting and raiding. I used to take them in, heal them, feed and clothe them, put them to work. Always, within a matter of weeks, they would steal all they could and head back to the hills killing any who tried to stop them. That is where I learned the use of primitive weapons – I hoped to earn their respect and allegiance by besting them at their own skills. I failed. Now we shoot them on sight.'

A decanter and glasses stood on a side table. Rolfe rose, crossed to it, poured himself a drink, and stood sipping, his eyes thoughtful as he stared at the instruments of death and their victims all around. He remembered a story a guide had once told him, of a bitch who had suckled a wolf and reared it as her own. But the wolf had never become a dog. It had reverted, killing the bitch and running back to the wild. Could a man do the same?

Quietly he said, 'Your suggestion, cousin?'

'The boy is not to blame and should not be penalised,' said Thurston quickly. 'But equally, he will never be happy on Joslen. Nor would he be content on any really civilised world. I suggest a holding be purchased for him on some frontier planet. A farm and buildings together with a fertile woman as his wife. Once he has children he will have a reason to stay. And his need to fight will be absorbed in the battle against the predators and elements.' He smiled, reaching for another capsule. 'But there is no hurry, cousin. A few days cannot matter. Think about it before you decide.'

'Now!' said Hardin.

Leon dropped his hand to his belt, lifted it, the primitive missile-weapon spouting flame and lead. At the far end of the range, clay discs shattered to left, right and center.

'Good,' said the instructor as the firing ceased. 'Eight hits and two misses. A quarter-second from word to first shot. However, that shot missed, and so didn't count. It is useless to fire unless you can also shoot straight. Now reload and try again. This time draw on the flash.'

He reset the timer and stepped back as Leon stood, tense as he waited for the signal.

'Relax. It is impossible to maintain a high pitch of tension at all times. To draw and fire must become a conditioned reflex. You could be walking through a jungle filled with predators which could attack at any time. To hold a gun and remain constantly alert would result in a reaction which could cause your death. You would become tired, your senses dulled and, when danger struck, you would be just that little bit too slow. You understand?'

'Yes,' said Leon.

'I wonder if you do?' said Hardin and then, in a different tone of voice, 'Is this yours?'

Leon turned with automatic politeness, caught the flash of the signal, and turned back to face the end of the range, firing as he moved.

'Bad,' said Hardin. 'But not too bad. I will set the range on random automatic. Reload and continue to practice.'

He moved from the firing step, a tall man with a thin, intelligent face creased with wrinkles about the eyes. He had devoted his life to the study and mastery of individual weapons and yet had never killed a living thing. Sometimes he doubted whether he ever could. To talk about it, to fire at facsimiles, was one thing. To see real blood spurt from real wounds, to watch a man or creature die, was something else. Yet he was the best tutor on Joslen and all who sought to fill their trophy rooms came to him for instruction.

He moved along the range, pausing to give advice, patient with a rotund man who complained about a bruised shoulder.

'The recoil is unavoidable and can only be controlled by setting the weapon firmly against the flesh. Hold it tight, cheek firm on the stock, butt hard against the shoulder.'

'These primitive guns!' The man was annoyed. 'Why can't I use a laser?'

'You can and will,' said Hardin patiently. 'But you did ask to be taught the use of a rifle. Once you have mastered that, the rest will be simple.' He called to an assistant. 'Bring cartridges with smaller loads. The recoil will be less,' he explained to the customer. 'You could use a small-bore rifle but I would like to get you used to the weight and handling of a heavier weapon.'

He moved on, dissatisfied but not showing it. So few were dedicated, most sought only to gain a little skill, and for most the guide would do the killing after they had fired and missed. Still, it was not for him to complain. He turned again to Leon and saw that he was not alone. Cyd Dee Thurston was with him, smiling, gesturing at the targets.

'So we meet again, Leon. Would you indulge me in a test of skill?'

It was two weeks since they had met at the party and Thurston was becoming impatient. It was a small matter, but to fail would affect his reputation and he had no intention of failing. Rolfe must rid himself of the boy and, if he would not, there were other ways. Yet always it was wise to know the enemy, young though he might be.

'Why not?' said Leon. 'Pistols?'

They fired and Thurston won. He was slower on the draw but more accurate, firing with a casually deceptive indifference.

'Practice,' he said. 'On Elgar I had plenty of time to indulge myself. Where you have been shooting for months I have been shooting for years. Shall we try rifles?'

This time Leon had the edge.

'Your eyes are young and sharp,' said Thurston. 'It helps to see at what one aims.' He put down his weapon. 'But this is child's play. How are you with cold steel?'

'Knives?' Leon frowned. 'You can throw a knife?'

'Not throw, and not a knife. A rapier. You have used the weapon? Good. Let us have a friendly bout. I'm sure that Hardin can arrange it.'

Leon was thoughtful as he followed Thurston from the firing range into the gymnasium. Instinctively he recognised the other man's dislike and wondered at the cause. He was Family, of course. Charisse had explained the relationship. But could that be the reason? Is was possible, he decided. The Dee's were a strong clan and could well resent outsiders. Or it could be a personal antipathy. If so, it was mutual.

Thurston crossed to where a rack of swords gleamed bright against a wall. Selecting two he offered their hilts to Leon.

'Take your pick,' he said. 'I give you the choice.'

'A moment!' Hardin came quickly towards them. 'Those are real swords, display weapons and not for use. They have no shields on their points.'

'We need none.' Thurston was casual. 'Nor masks or other protective clothing. We merely wish to test our skill and to be protected would be to lose the zest.' He appealed to Leon. 'You agree?'

Leon hesitated, instinct urging him to caution. 'Well, I –'

'Of course, if you are afraid, that ends the matter,' said Thurston quickly. 'I understood that you were skilled in the use of cold steel. Apparently I was misinformed. Anyone can be brave when there is no danger of getting hurt.' Air whined as he slashed it with his rapier. 'Well barbarian, do you admit to a lack of courage?'

'I cannot permit it,' said Hardin. 'Suppose one of you should be injured?'

'I absolve you from all blame.' Thurston did not take his eyes from Leon where he stood, sword in hand. 'On guard!'

His attack was a blur of motion, the point rising to stab at the eyes, light shimmering from the polished metal. Leon backed, his own weapon rising, clashing as it parried the other, lunging forward in automatic riposte. Thurston beat it aside, feinted, disengaged and lunged, his point barely touching the sleeve of Leon's jacket.

'Touché!' The older man backed, smiling. 'You must do better than that, barbarian!'

He attacked again, calmly, confidently, a cat playing with a mouse. The blades met with a thin high-pitched ringing, parted, met again, Thurston's following Leon's in a glittering counter-parry, vanishing to return, a shaft of brilliance, as he lunged in second. Again the point broke threads on the jacket, this time over the heart.

'Enough!' Hardin stepped between the opponents. To Thurston he said, 'I think you have proved yourself to be the master.'

'With two hits?' Thurston smiled with a flash of white teeth. 'The barbarian was unprepared, frightened, perhaps. I must give him his chance to take revenge.'

'Leon?' The instructor was undecided.

'Let us continue.'

Leon tensed as Thurston lifted his blade. The man was fast, with the conditioned reflexes of long practice, and he had the advantage of age, rank and position. If he hurt Leon it would be a regrettable accident, but if Leon were to injure him it would be a proof of his ingratitude. As the younger man he should have known better than to take advantage of the older. No one would pause to compare their relative skills.

He backed as the swords met, trying to remain calm, to remember his lessons. It wasn't easy to do. He was faced with naked steel and every instinct urged him to destroy the opposition before it destroyed him. And it meant to do just that.

Looking into Thurston's eyes he realised the motive behind the exhibition. It wasn't a simple test of skill at all.

The man meant to kill him in cold blood.

There was no time to reason why. There was no time for anything but to lift his blade and parry the attack, to back, to feel the rising tide of anger triggering his will to survive. His eyes narrowed and his mouth grew hard, cruel, aging his face and giving it the appearance of a savage animal. The blades rasped, glittered, needle-points winking like stars. Confidently Thurston pressed forward, disengaged, feinted, disengaged again and thrust, his point aimed directly at the heart. Not, this time simply to touch, but to plunge deep into living flesh.

Leon twisted, felt the point tear at his chest, saw the taut face and cold determination in the eyes of the man against him. In a normal bout he would have lowered his sword and acknowledged the hit. But this was not a normal bout.

Stepping back he lifted his sword and slammed the point directly at Thurston's chest.

'He tried to kill me.' Thurston lifted his hand and touched the bandage wreathing his upper left arm. 'He aimed straight for the heart and his eyes held death.'

'An accident.' Rolfe was disturbed. He looked at his cousin in the bed and felt the sudden need of a stimulant. The spirit was flavoured with cloves and aniseed, warming, giving a transient strength.

'It was no accident.' Thurston was grim. 'If I had not taken the precaution of wearing a protective garment I would be dead now. The mail deflected the point so that it tore my arm. But think, Rolfe. I had hit him. By all the rules he should have yielded victory. Instead he tried to kill me.'

'But why?'

'I told you why. He is intractable. It is his barbaric nature. Hurt him and he will hit back regardless of the consequences. And I am not talking about merely physical hurt. He could be bested in a commercial transaction and his reaction would be the same. Can you imagine such a man entrusted with delicate negotiations between powerful Families?'

Rolfe poured himself another drink. He was no fool and knew better than to take things at their surface appearance, but the fact remained that they had fought and both had been injured. The injuries were minor, true, but injuries just the same. And Thurston had hit first. Had he tried to kill Leon? And, if he had, would he try again? The use of assassins was not unknown to the Families, though always frowned on as an admission of failure.

And it was true that Leon had tried to kill in turn. Of that there could be no doubt whatever. Was the wolf beginning to show its fangs?

Shrewdly Thurston said, 'One thing puzzles me. Leon appears to have no regular woman. Could it be that he fears to upset Charisse?'

'What do you mean?'

'Nothing, cousin. It was a thought, nothing more.'

'Charisse looks upon Leon as a son.'

'Of course.' Thurston snapped a capsule between his fingers. 'But does he regard her as a mother?' Delicately he inhaled, his eyes watchful as he sniffed the fragrance. 'It would be a mistake to credit him with attributes he does not possess. A mistake as bad as to assume he wants to stay on Joslen. Perhaps you should give him the choice, cousin. Time grows pressing.'

Rolfe found Leon in his chamber. He stood before the open window staring at the city below. The room was in darkness and the external lights threw a diffused glow over his face. Watching him, Rolfe was reminded of an idol, impassive, full of hidden mystery.

'Rolfe?' Leon turned at the sound of the closing door. 'Is Thurston well?'

'Scratched, nothing more.' Rolfe crossed the room to join the other at the window. 'You made a mistake, Leon. A bad one.'

'I made two. The first was to have fought with him at all. The second was not to have thrust at naked flesh. I shall know better the next time.'

'There will be no next time,' said Rolfe sharply. 'A man should not fight unless he is able to control his temper.' He looked through the window. There was a soft wind which blew coolly against his cheeks, but far below in the cavernous streets, the heat would be stifling. 'Why are you standing in the dark?'

'I was thinking,' said Leon. 'Remembering. Do you know that once I restored sight to a man? I did it with a needle. It seemed at the time a wonderful thing to have done. Now it is not so wonderful. There are no blind on this world, no cripples, no diseased. Tell me,' he gestured at the city below, 'how is it that you have so much and Rhome has so little? Why cannot you share?'

He already knew the answer. There were too many worlds. Countless numbers of them spread throughout the galaxy, some rich, others poor, a multitude of diverse cultures. Inequality was inescapeable. But, Rolfe realised, knowing it did not help Leon to understand it. Only time could do that and he had lived so short a time.

And yet was that wholly true?

Rolfe frowned, thinking about it. How many men had crammed into their lives the experiences Leon had known? How could he be expected to fit into a mould fashioned for others? The Family were afraid of his intractability, his wild genes, the aggressive nature which was the heritage of his barbaric culture. But were these such bad things? Men were not sheep and new blood would bring new strength. Leon could provide that strength.

Quietly he said, 'Tell me, are you happy with your life?'

The answer was too long in coming. 'Yes, Rolfe, of course I am.'

'You don't think it dull? Monotonous? Isn't there anything else you would rather do?'

'To travel,' said Leon automatically. 'To see other places, other worlds.' He turned, smiling. 'I spoke without thinking. It was an ambition I had as a child.'

'And still have?'

'Yes.'

New blood, thought Rolfe. The eagerness and drive which had made the Family great. If he could not be adopted, at least he could be employed. Thurston must be made to see the advantages in such an arrangement, and so must the Family. He would insist they did. As a Manager of Joslen he had both influence and prestige. If they refused to cooperate he would appeal to the Director himself. He could even start a new branch of the Family.

Head buzzing with ambitious plans he left the boy's room, moving quietly down the corridor to pause at his wife's chamber. She would be interested in hearing what he had decided and might even be able to make constructive suggestions. Of one thing he was certain, she would do all in her power to promote Leon's welfare.

'Charisse?' He stepped softly into the shadowed chamber. 'Charisse? Are you asleep?'

She moved restlessly on the wide bed, turning to snuggle the pillow at her side, uneasy in her slumber. He reached out to touch her shoulder and she caught his hand, pressing it against her cheek.

'Leon,' she murmured. 'My darling! My own, sweet, dearest darling!'

Rolfe pulled free his hand and stared down at her, the blood draining from his face. It was obvious who filled her romantic dreams. But, he assured himself, as yet it could only be a matter of dreams. Even so, her subconscious had betrayed her secret desires. How long would it be before those desires overcame her, made her turn to Leon, not as a surrogate mother but as a willing mistress?

And what would the barbarian do then?

Thurston looked up as Rolfe entered his room. 'Cousin! You look ill! Is anything wrong?'

'Nothing.' The decanter made a rattling sound as Rolfe helped himself to a stimulant. Looking at the glass he said, 'I have been thinking and I have decided. It would be best for the boy to go.'

'As I suggested?'

'Yes, yes, I leave the details to you. Tomorrow I shall take Charisse on a short vacation. When we return the boy must be gone.' He drained the glass. 'And it would be best if neither of us were to know where he could be found.'

FOUR

Winter came early that year. For a week freezing wind screamed from the north scumming the ponds with ice and blackening the ripening grain. With it came a bank of sullen cloud, which covered the sky with the threat of early snow. When the wind died down Leon went out to inspect the desolation.

Little could be saved. The grain was flattened, blighted, and the root crops little better. With men and machines it might be possible to save something from the ruin, but he had no men, no machines, and little money to hire them from the village. If anything was to be done he would have to do it himself.

Grimly he continued the inspection, feeling a mounting anger, a savage frustration at seeing the sweat and toil of a year turned into waste. Of more than a year. He had been on Pharos for three.

He paused, looking back over the fields to where the cabin hugged the ground. It was strongly built of stone and timber, shutters protecting the glass of the windows, the shutters open now to admit the sunlight. From the chimney rose a thread of smoke pale against the leaden hue of the sky. Beyond the cabin stood a barn, almost empty now, and seven horses that blew vapour from their nostrils as they nuzzled at the frozen dirt of the corral beyond the stable. They at least he could sell, but if he did, how would he manage in the spring?

Irritably he strode over the ground, work-hardened muscles bunching beneath his leather clothing. To blame the elements was futile; to blame his own ignorance little better. To farm was basically a matter of preparing the soil, of planting seed, of fertilising, weeding, spraying and of patient waiting as the crops grew to maturity. The first year he had barely managed. The second spurred by a grim determination, he had enlarged the holding and taken a chance. Winning, he had grown even more ambitious, working from dawn until dusk, hoping to reap a rich harvest and, with the money so earned, to expand even more.

Now the gamble had failed and he was back where he'd started.

'Leon?' Shamara called to him as he entered the cabin. She came from the kitchen, a broad-hipped, big-breasted girl two years older than himself. A native of Pharos, she had thick blonde hair and a round, placid face dotted with little freckles. Her body was swollen heavily with child. Twice she had miscarried but this time she was confident she would bear him a son. 'Is it bad Leon?'

'Bad enough. The grain is ruined but we'll be able to gather enough roots to see us through the winter. And I can always hunt.'

'Must you?' Her eyes darted to where the heavy rifle hung against the wall. 'I worry when you are out hunting. Suppose you missed, or fell and hurt yourself? You could die out there in the wilderness and no one would ever know.'

He smiled at her concern. 'You worry too much.'

'I've reason to worry. My brother died while on a hunt, and so did my uncle. Furs and flesh aren't worth a human life.' She took his hand and rested it against her stomach. Beneath his palm he could feel the kicking of the child. 'And I need you. We both need you. Leon, you must promise to be careful!'

He turned to hide the impatience in his eyes. Shamara had come with the holding, an arranged marriage because, on Pharos, no man could farm alone. He had accepted her as he'd accepted everything else, because he'd had no choice. And she made a good companion if, at times, a cloying one. Three years had enhanced rather than diminished the adoration she felt for him, her pride at having won so handsome a man.

'Leon!'

'I'll be careful,' he promised. 'And you must be the same. You are close to your time. I think you'd better go into the village and rest at the infirmary. You work too hard in the house.'

'And you? What will you be doing while I'm gone?'

'Working, what else?'

'Cooking? Making the bed? Cleaning the house?' She smiled and reached up to wrap her arms around his neck. The swell of her belly made the posture awkward. 'That's woman's work, darling. And I've plenty of time. Your son isn't ready to enter the world just yet.'

'He'd better hurry,' said Leon, matching her mood. 'I can't work the farm much longer alone. I'll be glad of his help.'

'His and the others to follow,' she whispered. 'Darling, was any woman ever as lucky as me?'

'Lots of them,' he said bleakly. 'On other worlds –'

'But I don't want to be on another world,' she interrupted. 'I don't want to live in a big city with the stink of machines. I just want to be here, on Pharos, with you.' She pressed against him, the heat of her body demanding, urging. 'Please,' she whispered. 'It can't hurt me darling. I know it can't. And I need you so badly. I need you!'

Later, lying in the soft comfort of the bed, watching the glimmer of firelight on the boards of the ceiling, Leon had time to think of her philosophy. Was she so wrong not to want the mechanical comforts of civilisation? On Joslen he had been discontented, knowing himself to be out of place. Here, in conditions as primitive as those on Rhome, at least he should feel at home. And yet he did not. He knew too much. Each time he sweated in the fields he thought of the devices which could have saved him so much labour. Not the primitive machines available in the village, but the robotic harvesters common on civilised worlds. There men didn't bake in the sun or freeze in winter. They didn't burn wood for heat and light. Life, on such worlds, wasn't a matter of eating and breeding.

He fell asleep and dreamed of Thurston, the soft, vicious voice of the man as he explained what was to be, seeing again the narrowed eyes, the face, the shocked expression when he had sent the sword directly at his heart.

And woke to the screaming of horses.

'Leon!' Shamara reared in the bed as he dressed, wide-eyed, the full mounds of her dark-nippled breasts heavy against the swell of her belly. 'Leon! What's the matter?'

'The horses.' He snapped fast the buckle of his belt, slipped a knife into his boot and reached for the rifle. It was a simple bullet projector with a ten-shot magazine. He checked the loading, thrust fire to the wick of a lantern and headed for the door.

'Leon! Wait. I'll –'

The slam of the heavy panel cut short her words. Outside it was dark, the lowering cloud killing the light of the stars, the lantern throwing a pool of brightness. The horses were stabled in a building protruding from the barn, a low shed from which bars made a corral about the ground on which they grazed. He heard the screaming again as he ran towards it, the stamp of hooves and a low, feral snarling. At the edge of the pool of light something moved, eyes shining brightly yellow before vanishing, a grey furred body slinking to one side.

Leon reached the corral climbed the bars, ran towards the stable. Half-way there, something smashed into his back felling him, the lantern flying from his hand to land on the ground, flame rising from the spilled puddle of oil. In the dancing yellow light he saw a whiskered muzzle, the flash of gleaming fangs, a paw uplifted, bright with sickle claws. He rolled as they swept towards his face, the talons ripping clods of dirt from the ground, the predator snarling with baffled fury. He rolled again, felt the rifle dig into his side, snatched it up as he rose. As the beast lunged towards him he fired, fired again, a third time, the roar of the explosions echoing from the barn. The impact of the slugs flung the animal down and to one side, where it lay, blood gushing from the whiskered mouth, paws ripping the ground in dying fury.

'Leon!' Shamara called from the open door of the cabin. 'Leon! Are you all right?'

'Get back!'

'But –'

'Damn you, woman! Do as I say!'

The light from the burning oil was dying. From within the stable a horse screamed again and wood splintered beneath a lunging body. Dark shapes raced past, hit the bars of the corral and smashing them, plunged through. Leon ran to the side of the low shed and peered inside. He could see nothing, but heard a tearing noise, a wet slobbering. Cautiously he reached into the stable and felt straw beneath his hand. Grabbing a large handful, he twisted it into a bundle, ran back to where the oil still burned and lit the crude torch. The burning straw in his left hand, the rifle in his right, he returned to the stable. In the dancing light he saw the gutted body of a horse, another lying further within. From it, muzzle stained red, rose the snarling face of a predator.

Dropping the burning straw, Leon raised the rifle. The first shot missed, the second hit the lunging beast in the chest, the third smashed between the glaring eyes and threw the hundred and fifty pound carcass back on the corpse of its prey.

With his boot Leon scraped the burning straw into a small pile and added fresh fuel. He hoped the wind wouldn't rise and scatter burning sparks through the building. If it did the straw would catch, the stable itself, and, inevitably, the barn. But the risk had to be taken light was essential for what had to be done.

Cautiously he moved past the stalls the rifle ready in his hands. Crazed with terror, the horses had smashed down the partitions, and broken wood and scattered straw, most of it stained with blood, littered the floor. All the horses had escaped, other than those lyind dead, a thick trail of blood running along the ground showing that at least one of them had been badly mauled. He heard a scamper, the movement of a small body, but it was only a rat attracted by the scent of blood. He killed it with the butt of the rifle, tossing the body into the open, and continued his search.

There were no other predators. He checked again to be sure and then, throwing the bundle of flaming straw into the corral, he stamped out the fire he had built within the stable. He did it carefully, setting aside the rifle and scraping the dirt with the edge of a spade. By the time he had finished the straw outside had died to a patch of glowing embers. He stamped them out, eyes wide as he searched the darkness. Shamara had lit the lamp inside the cabin and opened the shutters so that a soft glow came from beyond the barn. He circled towards it, ears strained for the pad of paws, the rasp of feral breathing. As he approached the door opened spilling a flood of light.

'Leon?' She stood just within the opening, a loose robe tied about her swollen waist, the mane of her hair a shimmering golden stream about her shoulders. 'Leon?'

He sucked in his breath. Planet-born, she should have known better than to expose herself to possible danger. Predators hunted in families. One had waited outside the stable while the other fed, but they could have bred, and in that case—

He caught the gleam of greyish fur, the flash of light reflected from eyes at the edge of brightness. He began to run then dropped to one knee, lifting the rifle as he called to the woman.

'Back, Shamara! Back, for your life!'

He fired at the hint of movement. Grey fur shifted, became a solid shape, long and lean as it sprang towards the open portal. He fired again and saw wood splinter from the jamb. A third time as the door began to swing shut and saw the beast knocked to one side, the whiskered head turning to bite its hindquarter. Then, before he could fire again, the beast had lunged against the closing door, slamming it back on its hinges.

'Shamara!'

Leon rose, running, breath sobbing in his throat as he forced his legs to kill distance. From within the cabin came a scream, the sound of something falling, the wet meaty impact of a taloned paw. He reached the open door and, taking careful aim, fired the remaining shot. Dropping the rifle, he snatched the knife from his boot and threw himself to where grey fur tangled with white flesh, both fur and flesh bright with the crimson of freshly spilled blood.

The bullet had been enough. The steel he plunged again and again into the half-grown predator stabbed only dead meat. Meat which wore grey fur and which covered the disembowelled body of his wife, the mangled remains of his son.

The factor was kindly but firm. 'I'm sorry, Leon, but the contract is specific. The land is yours, but it cannot be sold until you have held it for ten years. If you should abandon it, it reverts back into the common pool.'

'I see,' said Leon. 'So I get nothing?'

'Not if you leave.' The factor hesitated. 'But must you go? You've worked hard and well and would be a credit to Pharos.

Shamara was a good woman and I know how you must feel, but there are other women and you would have no trouble in finding a wife. Can't you change your mind?'

'No.'

'Why don't you think about it? For the winter at least. When spring comes you may feel differently.'

The factor meant well but he didn't understand. It wasn't because of Shamara that Leon wanted to leave. He had never really loved her but she had been good and kind and had meant well. It was the thought of the wasted years, the constant toil while his life slipped away. The universe was not restricted to a farm.

He stepped from the factor's office, feeling the bite of the wind against his cheeks, blinking as snow swirled into his face from the freezing air. It had been a long journey from his holding in the north, down through the villages to the one town which Pharos possessed. Three years earlier he had arrived here, bitter but willing to commence a new life. Now that life was over and he was eager to get away.

To leave meant he had to find passage on a ship, and without money that would not be easy. The journey from the farm had taken almost all he had, the proceeds of the sale of his gun and other portable items had not been large and, in winter, work would be scarce. Ships too, were scarce. Only one stood on the landing field at the edge of the town.

It was of a type he had never seen before and its condition was a disgrace. The sides were marked and scarred, stained with various colours and blotched with patches. Turrets held the launching tubes of missiles and the squat barrels of energy cannon. About it hung an air of decay and yet despite that, something of its original beauty still remained. The clean, utilitarian lines of a machine built and designed for a functional purpose.

It was a mercenary, a warship for hire, and it had landed at Pharos to take on essential supplies.

Leon decided to find the captain.

He found him in a tavern, a big man, jolly, filling the place with his roaring songs and shouts of mirth. Soft fabric, cunning cut, disguised his bulk, and gems glittered on his pudgy hands. A wide belt supported a holstered weapon, and though the belt was new the gun was not. He was free with his money calling for jug after jug of the local wine, throwing coins at the serving girls and grinning at their delighted squeals.

A showman, thought Leon. A bouncing extrovert full of apparent bonhomie. But he wondered how such a man could be the captain of a ship.

Around him listening to his boasting, drinking his wine, stood the youth of the town, working men, mostly, with a scatter of artisans and the sons of local dignitaries. To one side stood older men talking between themselves, frowning at the big stranger.

He drained his goblet and slammed it hard on the rough table. 'Drink up, my friends. Drink, and enjoy life while you can. Look at me – a cup of wine for any I choose, soft fabric on my back, not a stroke of labour in over a year and this belly never came from starving.' He patted his bulk as the youths pressed closer.

'It's a fine life, I tell you. A free life and a merry one. None of your grubbing in the dirt, freezing in winter, roasting in summer, starving when the crops fail. It's just a spell on watch, an enemy in your sights, the squeeze of a finger and money for spending.'

One of the older men said drily, 'Why don't you tell them the rest of it, Captain? The blood and pain and sudden death. The wounds and agony, the disease, the vile creatures, the times when you have nothing and the times when you have to beg for life? Tell them the whole truth while you're at it.'

'You know?' The big man turned to look at the speaker. 'How can you know? How can any farmer know what it's like to be a man and to be free? You talk of blood and pain – have you none of that on Pharos? No injuries? No disease? No predators? No bankers who demand the fruit of your toil and sweat? Always life is a struggle my friend. But some struggle harder than others and with less hope of a decent reward.'

'Scavengers,' snapped the man. 'What else are mercenaries? Troublemakers. Killers who murder for pay. The quicker you get off Pharos the better!'

Leon saw the sudden jump of muscle along the captain's jaw, the drop of his hand towards the gun at his belt. Then he laughed and shrugged.

'You talk like a man afraid, my friend, but what do you fear? That I shall persuade some of your tame cattle to join us? That we shall poison your air? That, perhaps, I shall hold up a mirror for you to see exactly what breed of coward you are?'

'Coward? You call me that!'

'You and those like you on ten thousand worlds. When danger threatens, do you fight or do you send for us? Mercenaries to do your killing for you, to suffer and die in your place. Let a ship of some envious world hang in your skies and you would soon plead for help from those who you profess to despise.' His hand slammed the table as an ugly murmur rose from those gathered around. 'Well, isn't it true? How else would we stay in business?'

Leon said, 'Captain, I think you should apologise.'

'Apologise? For being a scavenger?'

'For insulting the people of Pharos. This is a hostile world and cowards would quickly die. Also you are a guest here and courtesy demands tolerance.'

For a moment the big man hesitated, his eyes searching Leon's face. Then he smiled. 'You are right. If I have offended I express my regret. Blame the wine, which is remarkably strong, or blame the ignorance of a stranger, but overlook my discourtesy. Yet if any wish to join us, let him be at the field tomorrow at dawn. And now, my friends, more wine!'

Leon followed him as he left the tavern. The big man was seemingly impervious to the cold which frosted the houses and sent plumes of vapour from his mouth. As Leon touched his shoulder he turned, cat-like, the gun lifting from the holster to level at stomach-height.

'You,' he said thickly. 'Wasn't that apology enough?'

'More than enough.' Leon looked down at the gun. It was a heavy-duty laser, strongly built, made to withstand use and wear. 'And you were wise to give it. On Pharos men have their pride, the streets are dark at night, and even your gun would be of little use against a concerted attack.'

'They would kill me?'

'No, but you would remember the beating for years to come.'

'I've been beaten before,' said the big man. He holstered the laser. 'And attacked before. Your name?' He grunted as Leon gave it. 'I am Sergil Karsh, acting captain of the *Homunculus*. Are you a native?'

'No.'

'I thought not. I watched you in the tavern and you have a different stamp to the yokels. And few of the locals would think to be so diplomatic.' He gusted vapour as a blast of wind caught his huge frame and pressed the soft fabrics against the broad expanse of his shoulders. 'For that, at least, I owe you a drink. Let us get somewhere out of this damned wind.'

They found a place close to the landing field, a secluded nook squeezed between two warehouses, where a simpering girl served them with scented brandy, pouting when Karsh rejected her offer of more intimate relations.

'A willing girl,' he said. 'Ambitious and eager to please, but too thin and fragile for my taste. Your health, Leon.'

They drank, and he recharged the glasses. Now that he was no longer acting, Karsh had changed; no longer the bumptious extrovert but more the man of heavy responsibility. His bulk wasn't due to excess fat, but was composed of bone and muscle, the result of formative years spent on a high-gravity world. Looking at his brandy he said, 'So you want to join us. Well, a good man is always welcome.'

'I didn't say that. I asked for passage.'

'The *Homunculus* doesn't carry passengers. Every man is a member of the crew.'

'To stand watch?' said Leon drily. 'To squeeze a trigger? To live high and rich on the loot of worlds?'

'You don't believe me?' The big man laughed as Leon made no answer. 'You're smart and I like that. The old man was right. It's a hard life and a dirty one but there are compensations. Only a fool would expect to be handed them on a plate.'

'And if those fools decide to join you? Are at the ship at dawn?'

'We'll take them. All who show promise that is.'

'Untrained men?'

Karsh was grim. 'They'd learn fast enough. We can't afford to be gentle and the first action would take care of those who were slow to learn. Do I have to explain?'

'About that no.'

'About what, then? How we manage to stay in business?' Karsh leaned back in his chair as if about to give a lecture. 'It is a simple matter of economics. It is expensive in time, men and money to train a force of fighting men and keep them idle for long periods. Only fully-developed worlds with a high surplus of wealth can afford standing armies. Underdeveloped worlds, cannot, and the galaxy is full of them. So when they need to fight a battle, or to defend themselves, they send for a force of mercenaries. The principle is as old as recorded history. You hire fighting men to do the dirty work and when it's done, you pay them off and send them on their way. The mercenaries themselves?' He shrugged. 'They do it because they want to. Understand?'

'Yes,' said Leon. 'I understand. What are the conditions?'

'A uniform, arms, rations and basic pay – received when you get it, which is usually after it has been earned. You probably won't make a fortune, but you'll have some good companions, an exciting life and see a lot of peculiar worlds. There's always the chance of promotion and you could even get to command a ship of your own. That's the good side. The bad is that you may get yourself killed or crippled at any time. Like the captain,' he said bitterly. 'Alexi's been lying in his bunk for seven weeks. He's dying and I expect to take over full command in a matter of days. Twenty-three years as a mercenary and he's rotten with a fungus he picked up on Skreen. Well, that's the way it goes.' He emptied his glass in a single gulp. 'Can you fight?'

'If I have to.'

'Which means nothing. Have you ever killed a man?'

'Yes.'

'Good. The first time is always the hardest.' Karsh slopped brandy into his glass. 'You could make a fine mercenary. How are you with weapons? Can you shoot?'

Leon remembered a darting shape, grey against a pool of light, the rifle and the way he had missed. Three shots – and Shamara had died because of his bad marksmanship. Slowly he said, 'I used to think so once. Now I'm not so sure.'

'You've a reason for saying that. Tell me.' Karsh frowned as he listened. 'Darkness, a brief target in lamplight and moving as that. A gun with open sights and you in a highly emotional state. It would take an exceptional man to hit a mark in those conditions. Even a superb shot could miss.' Or one, he thought, who had a subconscious desire to do just that. 'You shouldn't blame yourself. These things happen. They are a part of the experience of life.'

'Some experiences I could do without,' said Leon bleakly. Death had always seemed to ride him close. Well, perhaps he should face it, defy it in a more blatant manner. 'Will you accept me as one of your crew?'

'Gladly.' Karsh lifted his glass. 'Just one last question to satisfy my curiosity. 'You're obviously no farmer, so just what are you?'

'I don't think I know.' Leon remembered Thurston's sarcasm, his sneering insults when he had told him that he was unwanted, that the pet had outlived its interest and that he was to be thrown aside. Told him from behind the shelter of two men, armed and ready to use their guns. 'But I have been called a barbarian.'

Karsh gulped his brandy and flung the glass to shatter against the wall.

'Welcome home, brother,' he said. 'So have we all.'

FIVE

On a bush an insect was busy fashioning its snare. Thin filaments shone like threads of silver as it bustled from twig to twig, instinct dictating the fine engineering, the division of stress, flexibility and maximum efficiency. A robot, thought Leon as he watched it. A protoplasmic device gifted with a single skill. If he were to break the web the creature would build it all over again. It would continue to build it until death or the change of season intervened. It was capable of nothing else, lacking imagination, reason and the ability to learn. But for that it could not be blamed. The tiny ganglion which served it as a brain was incapable of grasping anything beyond the small immediacy of its own world.

Like men? he wondered. They too seemed to follow an instinctive pattern. They found new lands, farmed, delved into the soil for mineral wealth, built houses and palaces, turned to education in an effort to broaden their horizons, but only learned to do the same old things in faster ways.

And, they too, were only capable of limited awareness. The tremendous majesty of the galaxy was lost on a man who had to spend the daylight hours watching the furrow from behind his plough. The concept of endless worlds, of even a single world, was beyond the appreciation of restricted senses. So men, for all their power to travel between the stars, still fought and squabbled over a few square miles of dirt. With worlds for the taking and lands unexplored, pride and stubbornness still blinkered their eyes.

The earphone in his helmet said, 'Able and Baker now in position. Charlie report.'

'In position,' said Leon. 'Set and ready to go.'

'Advance one hundred and fifty yards. No firing.'

'Understood.' Leon tripped a switch with his chin and relayed the order to the men of his command. In the scrub, behind and to either side, a score of men began to move forward up the slope of the hill. They were good men. They made no noise and remained invisible as they took advantage of every scrap of cover. With life as the stake, caution had become second nature.

The insect had completed its web. Leon backed, moved to one side, edged forward taking care not to ruin the delicate construction. High overhead, twin suns burned in the sky, one yellow, the other blue, their combined heat baking him in his armour. He ignored the discomfort. Four years with the mercenaries had taught him to appreciate relative values and because of his Klarge-induced insensitivity he could wear the metal and fabric better than most.

He froze as fire blossomed to one side. A second explosion followed the first, then a string of them, and from high up the hill, came the dull reports of mortars. Cautiously he resumed his advance. The defenders were firing blind, hoping to score with a wide-spread pattern of random shots, a practice which was both wasteful of ammunition and a clear indication of rattled nerves. Reaching the new position, he chinned the switch.

'Vardis speaking. Section Charlie report.' Nineteen voices echoed from the earphone. 'What happened to Jhacarte?'

'I think he got hit, sir,' said a man.

'Go and make sure,' said Leon. 'If he was sealed he should

still be alive. Go and –' He broke off as a voice grunted from the phone. 'Jhacarte?'

'Reporting, sir. One of those damned bombs landed almost on top of me. I guess I got knocked out.'

'Are you operational?'

'Yes, sir. Just got a headache.'

'Very well. Check your camouflage and weapons. Out.'

From the eye-slits of his visor, Leon studied the terrain ahead. On the summit of the hill the castle looked a solid mass of indestructible stone, the high watch-tower dark against the sky. Men moved on the parapet as he watched, and little gouts of smoke rose from the hidden mortars. More explosions roared, this time further down the slope of the hill. Idly he wondered if his concern over the insect had been wasted, whether the tiny creature was now a fleck of broken tissue. If so it was merely a prelude of what was to come when other, larger, masses of living flesh would be smashed into lifeless pulp.

Philosophically he settled down to wait. War, it seemed, was mostly a matter of waiting. First to get the job, then to get into position, then again before the attack. This would be the final one. A series of ruthless actions had cut down the enemy's forces and pressed them back to the stronghold. Soon it too would fall and the thing would be over. Then would come the settling, the release from tension, when the victors, those surviving, would cram a year's enjoyment into a few days. And then the waiting again.

With professional interest he studied the castle. A single nuclear device would turn the whole edifice into incandescent smoke, but nuclear devices cost money and, worse, they destroyed all they touched. Ka'mut had terrorised the land for a generation. He had exacted tribute on every crop grown for a hundred miles. He had been a festering sore in the heart of the Gincha Province of Queem and had beaten back every effort of the locals to eliminate him. Now he faced hardened professionals and it was hoped, by those who employed them, that his treasure would pay their fee.

So there would be no nuclear device to cauterise the stronghold. No easy but expensive way out.

But, thought, Leon, Ka'mut had been a fool. He had neglected to sterilise the approaches to his castle and so had left cover to be used against him. Instead of primitive mortars he should have invested in heavy-duty lasers. The slopes should have been sown with electronic instruments and mines.

The earphones broke the silence. 'Leon, Able and Baker report no casualties. You?'

Karsh sitting in his command post playing the dangerous game of chess which he had made his life.

'No casualties,' said Leon. 'Any change in plan?'

'No. At dusk we move in.'

Leon sighed. More waiting. They had moved in, the previous night, edged forward with the dawn and now had to roast all the rest of the day. Lifting his visor he took a drink of tepid water from his canteen and broke the seal on a slab of rations. Before eating he spoke to his men.

'Time out to eat. Odd numbers take the first fifteen minutes. After eating, sleep if you can. Normal procedure.'

The food was solid, taking time to chew and satisfying to the stomach. Before going into action each man would swallow a capsule of drugs which would generate immediate energy, robbing their metabolisms but giving strength when it was most needed. And it would be needed, thought Leon, again studying the castle. Those walls wouldn't be easy to take, even when breached, and inside the place would be like a warren. He wondered if Karsh would join the final assault. Most probably he would. The big man chafed at inaction and once the attack had been launched, the men engaged, there was little else he could do.

Dusk came as the blue sun followed the yellow below the horizon. As the shadows thickened, Leon checked his weapons and armour. He called the roll and made sure each man was sealed and ready. The capsule was in his mouth. He bit down on it, swallowing as he moved up the slope.

When they were half-way to the castle Karsh opened the attack.

Air sighed as missiles hurtled against the walls, flame and noise erupting from the parapets, the massive stone. Karsh's gunners were of the best. The watch-tower collapsed beneath a direct hit, blocks of stone flying to fall like shrapnel on the defenders below. The walls were more stubborn. A hundred feet thick, laminated with sand and clay, they were pocked but not penetrated. Leon halted his men. To Command he said, 'Concentrate your fire.'

Karsh was terse. 'Guide us. Ranging shot coming now.'

Leon watched. 'Lower by twenty feet.'

'Right?'

'Still too high. Five feet lower and move ten to the left. Right. That's it.'

A roaring hell blasted against the base of the wall as a stream of missiles vented their energy against the packed stone. From it cracks ran up to the parapet, to either side, while from the point of impact rubble cascaded to make a slope leading to the ragged orifice.

'All right,' said Leon. 'That's enough. Cease fire now, we're moving in.'

Support fire reached up from the other companies as they advanced, pinning the defenders on the parapet, laser beams burning cloth and tissue to smoking char. Robot-like in their armour, the attackers reached the breach and passed into the ragged opening. Broken stones and dust showered from above and from the far end came a blast of fire. Leon dropped as a laser beam turned his camouflage to ash, reflecting from the mirror-finish of the metal underneath. As he fell he tore a grenade from his belt, threw it, followed it with another. As the explosions echoed from the end of the tunnel he rose and charged forward, firing as he ran. Large-calibre slugs, primitive but effective in smashing opposition, sprayed from stone, ricochetting, tearing into yielding flesh. He changed clips as the gun fell silent, then fired again as he burst from the wall. More of his camouflage melted away and a slug hit his chest, scoring a long groove in his armour. He staggered from the impact, regaining his balance and fell as a machine gun cut loose, his head ringing from a blow to his helmet.

Hitting the switch, he said, 'Charlie has entered the castle. Bring up reinforcements.'

He rolled, pulled his knees up beneath him, rose to his feet. From nooks and slits in the facing walls the defenders poured down a stream of fire. His men answered it, working with a skilled efficiency, silencing weapon after weapon as they took time to aim. Some had fallen and one who had received a direct hit from a high velocity cannon, showed the ruin of a smashed chest through his broken armour.

More men came running through the tunnel, Abel and Baker eager to join in the fray. In a body, the assembled men ran deeper into the castle, passing narrow passages, emerging into an open area ringed with slitted windows.

'Scatter.' Leon threw two grenades and blasted a window from which came a hail of bullets. 'Clean out this warren!'

It turned into a shambles. Demoralised, faced by seemingly invincible men, the defenders threw aside discipline and raced for safety. Few of them made it. Laser fire, bullets and grenades cleaned out area after area until only the solid walls of the keep housed opposition. Gigantic in his armour, Karsh glared at it and then turned to Leon.

'We could smash it, but if we do we'll probably lose everything of value inside. Suggestions?'

'Hit it from the air. Blow open the roof and drop men inside.'

'We can't do that. They got the last plane while you were in the breach.'

'Then attack from below. There must be underground passages of some kind. Bring up portable launchers and smash open the gate while I lead a party to come up from the dungeons. Do it quickly before they've a chance to reorganise.'

A shivering prisoner showed them the way, writhing in the grip of Leon's metal-sheathed fingers. Twice he had to smash his way through walls of stone, and then, as Karsh attacked through the gate, he came up to smash the defenders from the rear. It was a repetition of the major assault. A dozen fires started where lasers struck and the air was filled with chips of stone and the screaming whine of ricochets the frenzied shouts of men and the relentless noise of warfare.

The relative silence, when it was over, could almost be felt.

Ka'mut was found in a bomb-proof shelter deep beneath the keep, a place built of thick metal with an escape route fortunately blocked. He was a tall man, ascetically thin, with proud eyes and nostrils, and the mouth and eyes of a fanatic. He looked once at the shambles of the room into which they fetched him, then sat, a regal figure in his robe of scarlet filagreed with gold.

Quietly he said, 'To the victor the spoils, Captain. I underestimated your ability. I had thought that my own men had blood enough and spirit enough to have beaten you. It seems that I was wrong.'

'You were wrong.' Framed in his helmet, Karsh's face was dewed with sweat. The uplifted visor gave him the appearance of a monstrously beaked bird of prey. 'A pity you did not realise it before. I offered to parley. You chose to fight.'

'Could I have done anything else?' Ka'mut gestured with his hands. They were long, thin, dulled with splotches and heavily ringed. 'I have my pride, Captain. Those soft fools who employed you would not have been gentle. Did you know that twice before I have faced men of your calling? Did they tell you that?' He laughed soundlessly at Karsh's silence. 'No, I do not think they had. It would have altered the price, would it not?'

Karsh said, stiffly, 'The contract was satisfactory.'

'I could make it even more so, Captain. Double what you

hope to receive. More. As much again each year for the next five years providing that you agree to work only for me. Enough wealth to make you and your men rich for life.' Ka'mut waved one ringed hand as he gestured to the dead and injured lying in the room. 'Think about it before you refuse. Today you are the victor, but tomorrow you may be begging for your life. Why not take advantage of my offer? Together we could rule the province. You could train my men in the arts of war. You would become nobles under my reign. Money, Captain, land and houses, soft women and docile retainers. What more could a mercenary desire?'

'Why should we take a part?' said Leon softly. 'We could take the whole?'

'Did I ask for your opinion?' Ka'mut glared his anger. 'Who are you to interrupt the councils of your superiors?'

'He is one of my commanders,' said Karsh shortly. What he says makes sense.'

'To take it all?' Ka'mut shrugged. 'What is all? This castle and what it contains? That you have already. But the rest? The crop that grows and keeps growing from the sweat of the ignorant, the tribute, the taxes, the payments of those who seek friendship? That I alone can reap. Come now, Captain. You are a sensible man. Surely we can reach a mutually agreeable settlement?'

The celebration had started at dawn, and now, at midnight, it seemed that it had only just begun. From his window Leon looked down at the garlands in the street, the coloured lights, the masked dancers whirling as they followed giant figures with grotesque heads, the musicians adding to the frenzy of carnival with the blood-stirring beat of drums and pipes, the clash of gongs and the shrill plaint of flutes.

A simple people, he thought. Happy at the defeat of an enemy. Celebrating a war in which they had taken no part and for which they hoped never to pay. The treasure of Ka'mut would do that. The loot was found in the castle, the value of which was exaggerated at every mention until the streets were full of men who hoped to receive a fortune as their share.

Sheep, he thought. Born to be sheared. No wonder the brigand had held sway for so long. Impatiently he turned from the window, closing it, shutting out the sound of gaiety and laughter. Such things had no place here. Running down the length of the room, beds held the price of victory. Men whose armour hadn't been enough to give them full protection. The injured and dying. The hurt and maimed.

Mercenaries who had gambled once too often and who had no reason to celebrate.

He paused by one of the beds, recognising its occupant, a grizzled veteran of his own company. His face was strained, sweating, body shapeless beneath mounded sheets. He had taken the fire of too many lasers, his armour blackening, absorbing the heat, his body seared and roasted within its metal shell. Incredibly he tried to smile as Leon stooped over the bed.

'It was a good battle, wasn't it, sir?'

Good? Leon said, gently. 'At least we won.'

'And that's all that counts, isn't it? Beating the enemy I mean. Winning. Staying alive. Proving who is the better man.'

He was dreaming, thought Leon. Delirious. Confusing his terms. What did a mercenary have to prove? He knelt, resting his hands on those of the other man, closing his eyes as he concentrated. Once he had been able to help the sick and hurt, but no longer. Now it seemed that his gift had left him. Perhaps because he was too much among machines, living among men who did not recognise anything they couldn't see or hear or touch, in a society which regarded sensitives as freaks.

Or perhaps it was because he was too steeped in death and the thoughts of death for any curative power to survive.

'I'm dying,' said the man. 'Dying.'

Leon opened his eyes, forced himself to smile, to seem

bright with confidence. 'That's rubbish. You're hurt, but you're not going to die.'

'You're lying,' said the man dispassionately. 'I've seen too many men die in my time not to know what's going to happen.' He coughed and choked on a mouthful of phlegm. 'A hell of a life,' he gasped, swallowing. 'Sixteen years of it and you can count the good times on the fingers of one hand. And I wind up with a laser beam through my guts. Cooked meat roasted in a can. And for what?'

'It's a job,' said Leon. 'One you're good at.'

'Crazy.' The man rolled his head, lips whitening with pain. 'Get out of it, boy. You're young and there's a lot waiting for you. Quit while you've got the chance.' His hands moved like a spider over the sheets, found Leon's, pressed with failing strength. 'You're smart. You're not some clod without sense, willing to be a moving target and getting yourself killed. Find a woman, a piece of land, settle down, raise kids, have something to show for having lived. Don't be like me. Don't throw your life away. You've only got the one, boy. You've only got the one.' His voice trailed into disjointed mutterings as his hand loosed its grip.

Leon rose, turned, called down the ward. 'Doctor!'

The man was a local, slim and almost effeminate, yet capable enough. He came bustling to the bed touched the flaccid skin, pursed his lips as he met Leon's eyes.

'There's nothing I can do,' he said. 'Nothing anyone can do. The man is dying.' His eyes moved, looked down the ward. 'A lot of them are dying. I can ease their pain, but that is all.'

The noise of the carnival blasted his ears as Leon left the ward. Outside, life and music made a savage contrast to the pain and agony he had just left. A girl, painted with red and green, her naked skin sparkling with stars and crescents of gleaming silver, thrust a goblet into his face, laughing as she urged him to drink.

'Join me, my hero! Drink deep and wash that grim look

from your face. You are too young to be so solemn. Drink and let us play the ancient game of love.'

She fell back, laughing, as he thrust her aside. A man, plump, and wearing a wreath of leaves plucked at his sleeve. 'Mercenary, I have a proposition to make. One tenth your weight in silver if you will accomodate a few select friends.'

More voices, a stream of faces, music like the pounding of a heart, the wail of pipes a surrogate scream of pain. Hysteria and euphoria ruled the city and not one of the celebrants spared a thought to the blasted and mangled flesh which had won them their gaiety.

Leon thrust his way through them, turned down a side street, followed a dark alley and found himself in a shadowed plaza. To one side glowed the lights of a wine shop and he headed towards them, entering a low room heavy with beams and scented with herbs. A knot of elderly men sat at a table sharing a bottle and they stared at him as he ordered and gulped down ten ounces of spirit. One of them called out as he lowered the empty glass.

'Young man, will you honour us with your company?'

They were a group of philosophers eager to learn, and interested in the tall young stranger. Leon sipped wine and felt himself relax a little. These people, at least, would not sing outside a room holding dying men.

'It was a hard battle,' he admitted in response to a question. 'Our casualties were high in dead and wounded. The defenders fought well.'

'They had cause,' said one of the men. His name was Tarven and his hands trembled a little as he poured more wine. 'Ka'mut was a hard task-master and, had he won, those who flinched from the engagement would have suffered. But tell me, how do you justify your trade?'

'A moment, Tarven,' said one of the others. 'You are being discourteous to our guest. We have reason to thank him.'

'True, but the acquisition of knowledge lies in the asking of many questions. I have never killed a living thing in my entire life. I have not eaten the flesh of any creature. I doubt if I could defend myself against an enemy who sought my life. Ka'mut was a thing to be despised, true, but are we any better for having employed men to destroy him? Men who had no cause to hate him, who are willing to kill for pay?'

Leon looked into his goblet, seeing flecks of sparkling brilliance flash from the surface of the wine. 'I was a farmer once and had to kill vermin. On other worlds I have met men who made it their job to exterminate such creatures. A predator is no less a predator because he walks and talks like a man.'

'And that is your justification?'

'I need no justification. I am a mercenary. Unless there were those willing to pay for my services I could not be that.'

'So the employer is to be blamed, not the employed.' One of the men leaned forward. 'An interesting concept but one which holds a basic fallacy. Guilt is not so easily shed or aggression absolved. Tell me, if I were to employ you to destroy a world, dust an entire planet with killing radioactives, would you accept the commission?'

'That is different.'

'Only in a matter of degree. Each man is a world unto himself. By destroying him you destroy the universe as he knows it. And if you do not hesitate to kill one man, why hesitate to kill more?'

'There are more ways than one to solve any problem,' said one of the other men who had remained silent up 'til then, 'Ka-mut, for example. A surgeon does not remove a leg to cure a boil on the ankle. He is selective and destroys the cause of the illness, not the result. One man, skilled, could have eliminated Ka'mut.'

'An assassin?' Tarven shook his head. 'Must we always turn to instruments of death to ensure a peaceful life? Isn't it possible for men to live in harmony? After all, what does a man need? Food, shelter, a woman to bear his children and so ensure his immortality. The means to expand his mental horizons and the friendship of his fellows. So simple a thing and yet so hard to achieve. Always there is greed and ambition, dissatisfaction and envy. Sometimes I think that Mankind is cursed and doomed to suffer endless anguish.'

'An interesting concept, Tarven, but one without a basis of fact.' A man poured out the last of the wine. 'To blame some unknown being for making us what we are is to absolve ourselves from guilt and to justify every harmful action. I contend that each man must be responsible only to himself. Our young friend here. He is a mercenary. He kills for pay. No one makes him do it and he can stop at any time. He is a creature of free will and can choose the path he takes as can we all. But I thank him for what he has done in ridding us of the curse of Ka'mut. I thank him and I drink to him, as should we all.'

They drank, and the talk turned to general matters, of the harvest, trade, the carnival, local politics and the treasure found in the castle.

'A vast amount,' said Tarven. 'Or so I have heard. Perhaps our young friend can give us the truth of it?'

'I don't know,' said Leon. 'I left to take care of the wounded and, as far as I know, it is still being counted.'

'At the castle?'

'Yes. We have it guarded.'

'And Ka'mut?' said Tarvin slowly. 'Do you have him guarded also?'

Rumours, thought Leon. The babble of a drunken mercenary, a few words said to a woman over wine, and the whole city hummed with speculation. Cautiously he said, 'Everything is under control.'

'I hope so. If he should escape, there are tribes in the desert who owe him allegiance. Men of his own calibre, bloodthirsty and cruel. In a few years it would all have to be done again. More young men burned and killed, perhaps you among them.'

Leon thought of the dead and dying he had left in the ward. 'He won't escape.'

'It would be a bad thing if he did.' Tarven rose. 'Well, all good things must end. I bid you farewell, young man. May good fortune attend you.'

Leon nodded as they left, then ordered another glass of the local spirit. The distillation seemed to have no more effect than water. He felt restless, disturbed by a vague disquiet, as if there were things he should not have left unattended. An uneasy feeling such as he had felt on Helgar when, during a minor engagement, hidden guns had blasted half his command to bloody ruin. He had been lucky then, instinct causing him to drop, a second before the batteries had cut loose but, he wondered, just how long could such luck last? Maybe here, on Queem, it had finally run out.

The pilot said, 'Where do you want to be dropped, sir? I can't get too near the castle because of the convection currents.'

Leon hunched forward in the cockpit of the glider. It was almost dawn, the ground below thick with mist, the wings and fuselage of the frail craft thick with precipitated dew. The pilot, a local, banked the machine and grunted his satisfaction as he found an uprising thermal. As they climbed he said, 'There's a flat space to the south about a mile from the edge of the slope. Will that do, sir?'

They came down with a slight bumping and creaking of wood and fabric. Jumping down, Leon helped the pilot to wind up the springs of the launcher and turn the machine into the wind. From the cockpit the pilot waved and Leon stepped back, watching as the stored energy of the springs kicked at the ground, flinging the craft forward and up. The wind was strong enough so that the pilot did not have to use his rocket-boosters, and after skimming low for a quarter of a mile, he abruptly soared, wheeling, catching the preliminary light of the blue sun on his painted wings.

Leon waited until he was out of sight and then headed towards the castle. The air still seemed to hold the reek of combat, the lower slopes torn by the mortar fire, scrub and dirt flung in wanton destruction. A guard yawned as he approached the breach, snapping to belated attention, eyes wide, as he recognised the visitor. A second guard within rested against the ruptured stone, obviously asleep. Leon ignored him as he made his way towards the keep.

'Halt!'

'Sub-captain Vardis of the *Homunculus*,' said Leon formally. 'At ease.'

'Sir?'

'A message for the captain. Is he in the upper chamber?'

'Yes, sir. I think so, sir. Shall I announce you?'

'No.' Leon jerked his head towards the breach. 'But you might wake up your friend. If I catch him sleeping again I'll report him for punishment.'

Little had been done inside the keep to clear up the mess. The dead and injured of both sides were gone, but that was about all. A litter of fabrics and furnishings lay heaped on the rugs, most of them stained with blood or broken, and a few guards stood sullenly on duty, resentful at having missed the fun of the carnival. They had compensations in their opportunity to acquire a little personal loot, but this they regarded as their right in any case. For them the strain of the battle had still to be eased with women and wine.

Karsh was not asleep. He sat on a low couch before a table bearing cakes and wine. Opposite to him Ka'mut watched, a living idol, his eyes flickering as Leon thrust into the chamber. Karsh rose, his broad face anxious.

'You! But what are you doing here? Is anything wrong?'

'I don't know.' Leon stared about the room. To one side stood chests filled with minted coins and gems, delicate fabrications of stone and precious metal, statuettes, cameos, necklaces, rings a glittering display of things of value. 'Yours?'

'Ours. We share, Leon, you know that.'

'The price of our agreed contract, yes. A little loot, perhaps. But it seems to me as if you intend to gut the castle.' Leon crossed to one of the chests and dipped his hand into the contents. A shower of women's jewellery dripped from his fingers. 'How many years did it take to collect this stuff? How many women were raped and murdered to provide it?'

'Does it matter?' The captain's face was hard. 'It's here, that's all I care about. The price of a new vessel. More. Enough money to set us so high that we can afford to pick our next job. Our chance to get out of the gutter, Leon. We'd be fools not to take it.'

'And our contract?'

'To hell with that!' Karsh paced the floor, scowling, impatient. He hadn't slept since the battle, and it showed. 'I'm sick of living on the edge all the time. I've had a gutful of clearing out nests of vermin for fat farmers who lack the stomach to do their own dirty work. Tired of fighting for fools who begrudge my pay. And there's more. Each time I go into action I wonder if it will be my turn. You've seen the injured. Do you want to wind up like them? Blind, crippled, disfigured, lacking money for regrafts and proper treatment. And for what? To make some soft swine live a little easier.'

Leon said quietly, 'What's happened, Sergil?'

'Nothing. I've just had time to think, is all.'

'You've had all your life to think. What's so different now?'

He looked at Ka'mut and knew the answer. The old man was shrewd with a thorough knowledge of men. He had played on the captain's secret desires and struck a responsive chord and, of the two, he was now the master. He smiled as he met Leon's eyes, a gemmed hand lifting to touch the lipless slit of his mouth.

'An idealist,' he said. 'Listen to him, Captain, and you will regret it. How often have you had such an opportunity? How long must you wait before another such chance is offered?'

'Words,' said Leon. 'What else have you to offer? Promises, in order to save your life.'

'More than promises,' said Karsh eagerly. 'We've been talking and what he says makes sense. We could establish ourselves here. I'm getting old, Leon, and it's time for me to settle down.'

'The only settling you'd do on Queem is to settle in a grave,' said Leon flatly. 'And it would be large enough to hold us all. I've been learning things about our friend, and if you trust him then you're as good as dead. He's using you, Sergil, surely you can see that?'

'No one uses me!'

Leon stared into the captain's eyes. The pupils were dilated, the whites bloodshot, little flecks of mucous filling the corners. Madness? Karsh had always before shown a cold determination, governed by logical considerations. Drugs? It was possible. He had eaten and drunk with Ka'mut, and one of the rings the brigand wore could easily contain a psych-affecting compound. Certainly the man he now faced was not the same one who had introduced him to a mercenary's life.

Stepping back, he drew his laser and aimed the weapon at Ka'mut.

'Your rings,' he said. 'Strip them from your fingers. Rest your hands on the table palms upwards. Do it!'

Ka'mut hesitated. Karsh said, 'Steady, Leon. I give the orders here.'

'Then give them. Make him do as I say.'

'There's no need for that. Now why don't you step outside and get something to eat? That's an order, Leon.'

'You're doped,' said Leon coldly. 'Out of your mind. I don't take orders from a fool.'

'Vardis!'

Ka'mut said, 'Kill him, Captain! Kill him now!'

Incredibly Karsh tried to obey. His big hand fell to his belt, lifted bearing a gun, his finger tightening as it swung level. Both he and Leon fired together. For a long moment the captain stood, his face blank, then he fell to his knees, continued falling so that his head struck the rugs with a dull sound, turning to show the seared hole between his eyes.

Leon looked at his right arm. From the sleeve of his uniform rose a thin thread of smoke and he slapped at it, feeling the pain from the shallow groove burned in the flesh beneath, the wetness of his blood.

To Ka'mut he said, 'Now it's your turn.' And fired once more.

A laser made no sound so there was nothing to attract the guard outside. Leon stared down at the bodies, thinking. Under the mercenary code he was guilty of mutiny, the penalty for which was instant execution. Karsh had been a popular officer and now there was no way to prove that he had been drugged. Leon stooped, picked up the captain's laser and wrapped Ka'mat's fingers around the butt before dropping it at his side. The brigand had gone a little crazy and had snatched Karsh's gun, killing the captain and wounding Leon before being shot dead. The fingerprints would support the story if anyone should be curious enough to question it.

But he did not call the guard. Instead he sat, looking at the dead captain, the brigand, the treasure piled in the chests. Light came from the high slits of the windows, the blue radiance gleaming from the artifacts of gold, the elaborate embroidery of the rugs. It touched Karsh's face, shone from his staring eyes so that they seemed to glow with renewed life. 'A chance,' Leon heard him say, the words deep in his mind. 'The opportunity of a lifetime. Money enough to rise high.' And another voice, thick with pain. 'Get out of it, boy. Get out of it.'

Good advice from men now dead.

He rose and crossed to the door, opened it, stepped outside. To the guard he said, 'You look fagged. Go and get something to eat.'

'Sir?' The man's eyes moved past Leon to the door.

'It's all right. Do as I say.'

He waited until the man had left then moved down the

stairs of the keep to where the radio-operator sat beside his instruments. The ship was guarded by a half-dozen men and an officer. Cline was dubious.

'Move the ship? Well, I don't know. It's a short hop and won't be easy.'

'If you can't do it, find someone who can!' Leon was curt. 'There's a flat place below the slope leading to the castle. I want to see you land there in thirty minutes.'

'But what about the rest of the men? They're still in town. I could never assemble them in time. I–'

'Leave them. You've enough to handle the ship and it's needed immediately. That's an order, Cline, direct from the captain. Now move, damn you!'

There could be trouble from Cline but he would handle it when it arose. In the meantime there were other things to attend to. Leaving the radio-room, he stepped from the keep and looked around. The castle was garrisoned by a score of men, many of them of his own command. Redfern, the commander, reared from his couch as Leon slammed into his room. He was a thin man with sparse hair and a scarred face, of the same rank as Leon but older, which give him seniority, and he was jealous of his privileges. He blinked and shook his head.

'No, Vardis, an order like that has to come from the captain himself.'

'It did. I'm relaying it.' Leon picked up the man's uniform and flung it towards the bed. 'The ship is to be loaded with everything of value this place contains. It will be here soon, so get up and get moving.'

Redfern donned shirt, pants and boots. With one arm in his jacket he said, 'What's the emergency?'

'We could be attacked by the tribes of the desert. They know Ka'mut is beaten, and could hope to pick up some easy loot. If it isn't here they can't do it.' He saw suspicion growing in the man's eyes. 'I heard about it in town and came right out. Karsh agrees that it would be best to safeguard what we've won. The only way is to load everything on the ship. Now stop arguing and move!'

'Not so fast, Vardis.' Refern slowly belted his laser about his waist. 'I think I'd better see Karsh about this. As far as I know he had different ideas.'

'He's changed them.'

'Maybe. If so he can tell me.'

'I'm telling you. See him if you want but at least get things moving.'

Refern was stubborn. 'There's no hurry. A few minutes can't make all that difference. I want to see the captain.'

Leon shrugged. 'Sure, why not? But don't blame me if he chews you out.'

He led the way up the stairs and along the passage to the closed door, stepping back as Refern knocked and thrust open the panel. It took him a moment to grasp the picture. Then he turned, his face working.

'Dead,' he said. 'They're both dead!'

'Ka'mut must have killed him. You can see what must have happened. He –'

'You're lying! There was no reason for him to have killed the captain. They'd worked out a deal. You!' His eyes narrowed. 'You did it! By God you're trying to grab it all. You —'

He broke off, snatching at his gun. Leon shot him before it cleared the holster and watched the body fall.

'That's right,' he said softly. 'And I'm going to get it.'

SIX

In the dimness she was a pearly gleam with midnight hair and arms like blind worms as they rose to clasp him about the neck. Her body was soft and warm, a symphony of curves yielding as they pressed, breasts and stomach and thighs, matching the softness of her lips as they sought his own with demanding insistence. Unresponsive, he lay supine, staring at the ceiling, conscious of her warmth and perfume, detachedly aware of the arrogance of her flesh.

'Leon!' Her nails dug into his back. 'You insensitive beast!'

'Is that all I am?'

'No. You're a gorgeous handsome, wonderful man, and I love you very much.'

Her hands moved, caressing his face, his hair, the slope of his shoulders and chest. Hair brushed against his cheek and one long thigh rose to press against the lower portions of his body. Her breathing came faster as her passion mounted and, he knew, soon that passion would be converted into anger if it continued to be frustrated by his indifference. At eighteen, Malinda Dee Strenach had not yet learned to be tolerant.

'Leon!' Again her nails dug into his flesh. 'Leon!'

He turned and reached for her, satisfying her demands with mechanical precision. She sighed and relaxed, snuggling against him, one hand lifted to stroke his cheek.

'Darling,' she whispered. 'You're such a wonderful lover. You make it last so long.'

'That's because I'm insensitive.'

'Really?'

'It's something I picked up when young. A poison which almost killed me. It affected my sensory nerves so that I require greater stimulation than a normal man. It's getting worse and one day will kill me.'

'Leon!' She rose and stared down at him. 'You're joking!'

'No.'

'You have to be! Please! Tell me you're joking!'

'All men have to die, darling, including me.' He smiled and saw her face relax. 'But it won't happen for a long time yet. Do you still want to marry me?'

'Of course, darling, but –'

'But the Family won't let you,' he interrupted. 'You know

it and so you didn't ask.' His voice sharpened a little. 'You didn't, did you?'

Malinda shook her head, hair wreathing her cheeks, falling over her shoulders and almost covering her breasts. She had nice hair and a nice body. He touched it, kissed certain sensitive areas, smiled and withdrew as she reached towards him.

'You're insatible. Didn't anyone ever tell you that a lady shouldn't be so hungry for love?'

'No, why should they?'

'Because a good salesman never gives too freely of his wares.'

'You –' He caught her hand as it swung towards his cheek. 'You – barbarian!' She smiled to show she wasn't really annoyed. 'You traders are all the same. Everything has to be costed on a profit basis, including love. Why can't you learn that some things have no price? I love you. I'm willing to give you everything you want – I do give you everything you want and, in return, you insult me. Sometimes I wish I'd never met you.'

But that was a lie and they both knew it. She had fired herself at him like a bullet from a gun, determined to win the rich prize he appeared to be, the tall, elegant stranger who had suddenly appeared in her society, his very mystery enhancing his attraction. She would never know that it was not her body which had attracted him, but her name.

Rising, he donned a robe and from a drawer took a glinting thing of gold and sparkling gems. He held it, allowing it to swing so that the subdued light caught the jewels and turned them into patches of living colour. She stared at it, a child entranced by a glittering toy, her eyes following it as he brushed his hand over a control and caused light to blossom into brightness.

'For me, darling?'

'For you.' He threw it towards her, watching as she clasped the bracelet around her slender wrist. 'Did you find out what I asked?'

'About Charisse Dee Bouchet?' Malinda shrugged. 'She's dead. Killed three years ago by an accidental overdose of sleeping pills. Leon! This is lovely!'

'Dead?' His voice was sharp. 'Are you certain?'

'Of course, darling. It's all in the archives.'

'And her husband?'

'Oh, Rolfe is still alive somewhere.' Malinda lifted her wrist to gloat over the trinket. 'Leon, you are so good to me. If I wasn't hopelessly in love with you already, I'd fall in love with you because you are so generous. Darling! Come back to bed so I can thank you!'

'Later.' Her demands bored him with their empty repetition. Like most girls of her class and age she thought that all she had to do to satisfy a man was to make herself available. The deeper, emotional significance of an intimate relationship completely eluded her. 'Could you find out where Rolfe is living?'

'I could, I suppose, but why, Leon? What interest can you have in him.'

'Business, darling. What else?'

'But he's old and must be retired by now. Anyway, he wasn't in commerce. He was a Manager of some planet, Joslen I think, administration or something. You'd have nothing in common.'

'Even so, I'd like to know. Will you find out for me?'

He could do it for himself but perversity made him use the girl. And it made her feel important and so all the more eager to help. In order to use people he had learned, it was essential to do that. To make them feel that they carried responsibility, were trusted, were offered a challenge which their pride forced them to meet. And, at the same time, never to let them know his true motives or his real interests.

Five years of commercial warfare had taught him that.

He crossed the room and threw back the curtains, disdaining the electronic device which would have done it at a word, in the impatient need of physical action. Late afternoon sunlight illuminated his face, gilded the roofs of the city beyond, threw great shadows into the cavern of the streets. To one side rose the glittering tower of the Jays, the great trading family of the sector, with whom he was negotiating. Beyond sprawled the complex of the medical center, next to it reared the bulk of the central computer, around and behind rested a maze of offices and high-income homes.

Moris, like Joslen, like any of a thousand other civilised worlds, followed the same pattern of evolutionary development. Clustered cities which grew too large to be economically viable, slums which rotted in their hearts, overstrained transportation and resources. Later would come the dispersal, when open space would separate dwellings and the ugly buildings would be snugly out of sight beneath the ground. But that would take another three centuries to happen here.

'Leon?' The girl was behind him, gossamer fabric veiling her body, accentuating her curves. 'What are you thinking about, darling?'

'You,' he said. 'Us.'

'Our future?' He felt the warmth of her body as it pressed against his back. 'I've been thinking, darling. We could go away somewhere. You have money, and we could settle on one of the primitive worlds. It would be fun. Darling, it would be so much fun!'

Fun! A thrill of the moment, playing the rich lady until the novelty palled and boredom took its place. Until she became a petulant child crying for the moon. He turned to face her and looked into her eyes.

'I was thinking of the ball tomorrow,' he said deliberately. 'What are you going to wear?'

'This.' She exposed her body. 'Just me, and paint, and a few spangles.' She saw his expression. 'No?'

'No. Every girl with a good figure will be doing just that. Be different.' He stepped back, studying what he saw. 'Your hair is good so leave it hanging loose. Accentuate your eyes and wear a thin veil. Then a simple dress, white trimmed with gold, leaving one shoulder and arm completely bare. Naked feet, and sandles also of gold. A belt of the same material.'

'A mess,' she pouted.

'True, but do you know why?'

'The veil and dress do not match.'

'Correct, so we will forget the dress. Instead, wear a short jacket, jewelled and barely covering your breasts. Loose pants of translucent material. The veil, of course, and the hair as before.'

'Barbaric.'

'What you people think of as being barbaric,' he said. 'Actually, barbarians do not wear anything like that. Clothes are worn to protect, not to allure, and an outfit like you'll be wearing would be useless against both sun and cold. But you'll be decorative, and you'll stand out against the mass of painted skin displayed by the others.'

'And you?'

'I'll come as a barbarian,' he smiled. 'What else?'

On Moris, business was of paramount importance, and so there was no nonsense about the hours in which it should be conducted. A shift system kept the city humming every hour of day and night, with artificial light replacing the sun. At dusk Leon moved from his apartment to the Jay Tower, a cab carrying him from his door to the entrance, an attendant ushering him into an elevator and up a hundred and fifty floors, another showing him into the palatial office of Shawn Jay Harmond.

'A pleasure, sir,' he said advancing to greet his visitor. 'One long deferred. I am happy to welcome the famous Leon Vardis to our tower.'

'You are too generous.'

Harmond smiled. He was a short, fiery man, who disdained artificial aids to retain his youthful appearance, his scalp unashamedly bald, his eyes glinting behind wide lenses, a ruff of grey beard trimming the line of his jaw. Even so, his step was springy and his hand, though mottled with brown patches, was strong as he gripped Leon's own.

'You'll take a little refreshment? I have some excellent wine and some honey-spirit I can recommend. A little on the sweet side, perhaps, so maybe you would prefer some brandy?'

'Brandy,' said Leon.

'A wise choice. I will join you.' Harmond poured the drinks, generous measures in fragile goblets 'Your health, sir!'

Leon touched the spirit to his lips, not swallowing, then examined the room as he set down the glass. Wide windows, curtained now, would give a fabulous view of the city. Frames held delicate paintings, embroideries, patterns built of fragments of insect wings, of slivers of stone, of gums and seeds and leaves like lace. On small tables stood various carvings, some of them startling in their unabashed obscenity, others like poems in crystal, songs in bronze. A hundred different items from as many worlds.

'Gifts,' said Harmond. 'Items of stock. Things which attracted my attention, or the attention of the one who used this office before me. Sometimes I have been urged to get rid of them, but as I always tell the bright young men with their new ideas about what an office should be, I like to be reminded of what we are and what we do. And, also, I like to look at them and think of other worlds. You are a travelled man, sir?'

'You know that.'

'Of course. You must forgive me, I am too accustomed to dealing with men who are reluctant to come to the point. You, I see, are not such a man. Good. Neither am I. So let us get down to business. First, we are interested in your proposition, but the terms—' Harmond pursed his lips. 'There, I am afraid, lies the stumbling block.'

'In that case,' said Leon coldly. 'I am wasting my time.'

'Not so! Let us look at the matter.' Harmond poured them both more brandy, ignoring the fact that Leon had not touched his previous drink. Sitting at his desk he set down the glass and rested his elbows on the polished surface. 'You first came to our attention five years ago when you suddenly appeared with a cargo of various items, all of barbaric manufacture and all acceptable to our luxury market. We agreed to handle them for you, and as a result, you received quite a respectable sum of money.'

'You took them on a basis of fifty per cent commission. We both made a lot of money.'

'True, but we had expenses. From our share came distribution, retailer's margins, book-keeping and the rest of it. You then continued to trade and now you are an extremely wealthy man.'

So?'

'It presents an intriguing situation.' Harmond gestured to the chair standing beyond his desk. 'Won't you please sit down? It makes me uneasy to talk to one who stands.'

The chair was undoubtedly fitted with electronic devices which would register the veracity of anyone sitting in it, but Leon did not hesitate to sink into the soft cushions.

'Thank you,' said Harmond. 'Now the proposition you have made to us is that we should finance the cost of an expedition to a planet you refuse to name. That is understandable at this stage of negotiation, but what is not is why you should seek our help at all. You have your own ships and men, and are apparently perfectly capable of undertaking your own venture.'

'So why do I ask for your help?' Leon shrugged and sipped at his glass. 'You have answered your own question. I am a wealthy man and intend to remain so. Risking everything on a single gamble is not a wise policy, as you well know. That is why I am willing to share the profits. Meet the cost and take half of what is found.'

'You talk of a large sum.'

'I talk of large profits.'

'They are speculative. We are a conservative Family and

have built our wealth and reputation on a basis of caution. There can be no certainty that the enterprise will succeed.'

Leon set down his glass and reached into an inner pocket. Quietly he said, 'We can be certain of only one thing. Each one of these is worth a small fortune.'

From the pocket he took a gem and rolled it across the desk so that it came to a halt before the other man.

It was as large as an egg, covered with a multitude of facets so that it caught the light and reflected it in a myriad of rainbow shimmers. Beyond the shimmers, buried deep in the heart of the gem, pulsed a node of scintillating brilliance.

'Take it in your hand,' urged Leon. 'Look at it. See the change of colour.'

Harmond sucked in his breath as he picked up the gem. He cradled it in his hand, and as he watched, the node grew to fill the entire jewel, so that his hand was filled with a sparkling glory of heart-stopping beauty.

'Look at it,' said Leon again. 'Concentrate on the brightness. See how it expands to fill your entire vision. There are pictures in the brightness, scenes from distant places, creatures of flame, cities with twisted spirals for towers and soaring arches on which are perched birds with plumes of crystal.' He waited and then reached out his hand and covered the gem. 'What woman could resist it? What man for that matter? I know where they are to be found, but they are not easy to get. That one cost a dozen lives.'

Harmond exhaled with a gushing sigh. Reaching for his glass, he swallowed half its contents at a gulp.

'I had heard,' he said slowly. 'The junior you first saw told me, but I didn't believe. I couldn't imagine such splendour.' He moved his hand from beneath Leon's shielding palm and again stared at the jewel. 'Hypnotic,' he said. 'It has to be. And your words triggered off suggestive chains of thought so that I could not help but respond. Where did you find it?'

Leon's face was impassive as he pocketed the gem. 'You agree to my terms?'

'Total finance for a half share? No.'

'Then you aren't interested. Well, no matter. If your Family is unwilling to take a chance there are others which will.'

'The Dees, for example?' Harmond's eyes were shrewd. 'I think not.'

'You have reason for saying that?'

'Only my knowledge of how they operate. The Dees are concerned mostly with factories and mines, agriculture and construction. They are not a trading concern. Now let us discuss terms. If we agree to finance the entire expedition then you will, in a sense, be in the position of a guide. I can offer you five per cent of the net profit.'

'Fifty.'

Harmond sighed, 'The jewel is superb,' he admitted. 'But if you held a vial containing the very stuff of immortality in your hand I could not agree to such terms. Think a moment. You ask us to risk a fortune, and in return, you expect to gain as much as we. You hold the secret of where to obtain the gems, true, but that is all you offer. And what is it that you really propose? You ask that we stand the cost of ships and men, the equipment they will need, the supplies. You could find nothing and still make a profit. You are a shrewd trader, sir, but we also are not without experience. Seven and one half per cent.'

'Net?'

'Of course. Or if you wish, we will market the gems for you at a twenty per cent commission.'

'Ten.'

'You are a hard man, sir,' said Harmond. 'But on that, at least we can agree. Providing, of course, that we are your sole distributors.' He punched buttons on his desk and handed Leon the paper which emerged. 'Our agreement and formal contract.'

Leon rose, folded the paper and slipped it into a pocket. Harmond too, rose, pleased at the way things had gone. Ten per cent of certainty was better than fifty per cent of a promise. As he had said, the Jays proceeded with caution.

A man, beaked and plumed like a monstrous bird, flapped stunted wings and squawked, 'Your name, sir?'

Leon gave it, heard it relayed to the rooms beyond, waited as it was checked against the list of those invited. A tall skeleton bowed as he was passed through the barrier, a naked girl puffed scented smoke into his face, a blotched creature of nightmare simpered and plucked at his sleeve.

'Read your hand, dearie? Tell your future?'

The rags were genuine, the sores, the disfigurations convincing. The organisers of the ball knew how to pander to jaded appetites, and had employed fifty unfortunates to provide titivation. A man hopped past on legs which ended at the knees, face grimed with dirt and repulsive with a seeping ulcer which was eating into his jaw. A mutant followed, black hair spiked on a massive hump, feet splayed and each with seven toes. An armless girl swayed past with teeth like fangs and hair which writhed and hissed.

Others shambled, stumbled, staggered and sprang in the vast confines of the ballroom, some with extra limbs, others with extra eyes, a man with a child apparently growing from his side, a woman with two heads, another with a multitude of pendulous breasts. Genuine? False? In the smoking dimness it was impossible to tell.

'Leon!' Malinda came towards him, painted toes peeping through the straps of her golden sandals, eyes grotesque above her veil. Possessively she clutched his arm as he moved through the crowd. 'I've been waiting for you. Why are you so late?'

'Business.'

'Again?' Her full lips pouted beneath the gauzy translucence. 'You're always thinking about business. Why don't you think of me for a change?'

'I think of you all the time,' he said patiently. 'Even when

I'm asleep.' He halted as a blind man tapped past, milky orbs staring upwards where balloons in the shapes of people mingled in obscene parodies of the erotic arts. 'But I have to think of making money too.'

'Lots of money?'

'The biggest fortune you ever saw. Just as soon as I can arrange a few things, I'll be off to collect enough money to buy a world.'

'Those jewels?' She shook his arm. 'The one you showed me?'

'I asked you not to talk about that.'

'I didn't. I mean – that is – Oh, Leon! You look so handsome!'

It was a clumsy way to change a subject, but she was a clumsy girl when it came to intrigue. And he did look spectacular dressed in red and gold, a long knife in his belt and a jewelled crest on his head. Unseen were the thin shirt of flexible mail he wore beneath the finery and the laser built into the crest, which could be fired by a contraction of the muscles of his scalp.

'My man!' sighed Malinda happily as she hung on his arm. 'Isn't this a simply wonderful ball, darling? All those freaks and things! I get the most delicious shudder every time I look at them.'

Drily he said, 'You should become a nurse.'

'A nurse? Why, darling?'

'Then you'd really have a chance to enjoy yourself. All those people smashed and crippled, diseased, disfigured, dying. You'd really have fun.'

'Leon!'

Immediately he was contrite. 'I'm sorry, darling, please forgive me. Has anyone here told you how beautiful you are?'

'Lots.' She smiled, annoyance forgotten, her mind too shallow to have grasped the full implications of his sarcasm. As a shower of crystalline flakes descended from above, melting, releasing nose-tingling odours and euphoric vapours, she came closer and pressed the mounds of her breasts against his chest. 'There was one old man who offered to pay me a tenth of my weight in silver if I would sleep with him. Would I be worth it, darling?'

'More than worth it.'

'How much more, darling?'

'Your weight in gold at least.'

'For a single night?'

'For a single hour.'

He moved into the rhythm of a dance before she could continue the stupid game, stepping back, jerking, moving forward in time to the pulsing beat of music designed to accelerate the heart and dissolve inhibitions. Overhead the mannikin balloons moved in a simulated frenzy of copulation, gouts of perfume spurting from tumescent organs. Leon ignored them, concentrating on the girl. Why was she acting so stupidly tonight? So transparently girlish and painfully young. She was both, but the veneer of her culture usually gave her a protective, if false, air of sophistication. Guilt, he decided. The little-girl act was to protect her from the fury of an adult, to disarm suspicion and to reveal how truly innocent she really was.

He found it amusing.

The dance ended and they ate from garlanded stalls, using their fingers to pick up succulent morsels from dishes served by a mechanical octopod. Coloured lights flashed about them in stroboscopic frenzy, writhing dancers performed acts of undisguised hysteria, a fire-eater screamed as he seared his lungs with a special fuel provided by the management for that exact purpose, a woman ate a living hen and spattered blood over those who watched.

An hour before dawn the cries of the unfortunates rose in a cacophony as they took advantage of the management's permission to beg. Malinda, face flushed above her veil, demanded money from Leon and went to watch a disfigured couple locked in a pitifully inadequate embrace. As the spectacle palled, she threw coins at the labouring pair and turned to seek fresh entertainment.

Leon caught her arm. 'I've had enough.'

'You want to leave? But, darling, it's early yet!'

'You can stay if you want but I'm going.'

She frowned, then shrugged. 'All right, if that's what you want. But I must freshen up first. Meet you by the entrance?'

He nodded, watching as she left, then moving to one of the stalls where he stood eating a dish of sugared snails. The man who approached him was dressed all in black and silver, spines glittering on his head, a grotesque mask covering all but his mouth. 'Your pardon, sir, but am I addressing the trader Leon Vardis?'

'You are.'

'Then would you be so accommodating as to accompany me, sir? There are certain gentlemen who seek a private audience.'

Leon put down the dish of snails. 'Their names?'

'Discretion forbids me to mention them in this public chamber, but I can assure you that they are of the highest quality. I can also assure you that you will be in no personal danger.'

'I accept your assurances,' said Leon. 'But I have arranged to meet a young lady. It would be impolite of me to let her wait.'

'She will be informed, sir.' Spines glittered from the knuckles as he lifted a hand to gesture to one side of the ballroom. 'If you are ready?'

'No,' said Leon. 'I am not ready. And I am not in the mood for mysterious meetings with mysterious strangers, no matter how high their quality. You may tell them that. You may also tell them that I shall be at home until this afternoon. If they wish to call I shall expect them at noon.' His hand dropped to the knife at his belt. 'Is something delaying you?'

At the entrance, Malinda said, 'Leon, darling, would you be very annoyed if I didn't come home with you?'

'Very annoyed.'

'But, darling, I have so many things to do! I've an appointment with my dressmaker and another with my cosmetician and I should really go for a dental check-up and I need a new contraceptive injection and –'

'You don't want to come home with me,' he interrupted. 'I understand.'

'Do you, darling? Do you really?'

'Yes,' he said. 'Really.'

He woke from a dream of flames and screaming to hear the muted chiming of the announcer. It was barely noon, and he felt hot and sticky from restless sleep. Rising, he thumbed the button activating the scanner. The face in the plate was that of a middle-aged man, rotund, smoothly clean and pink with massage. He said, 'Trader Vardis, my apologies if I have inconvenienced you, but there are matters we should discuss. May I enter?'

As Leon hesitated, his face left the plate to be replaced by that of Malinda's. She smiled, lovely in her freshly groomed beauty, neither eyes or skin betraying her lack of sleep.

'Darling,' she said. 'You're so cautious! I told daddy that you wouldn't let him in.'

'Your father?'

'Covis Dee Strenach, sir.' The man reappeared in the plate. 'Or should I call you Leon? We are, after all, very close.'

'Leon will do. Ask your daughter to serve refreshments. I will join you shortly.'

Leon activated the door and went into the bathroom to shower. Dressed, he moved through the apartment to the room where his visitors would be waiting. There was one more than he'd expected.

'So, Leon Vardis,' said Cyd Dee Thurston. 'We meet again.'

He had not changed. The passing of a dozen years had done little more than thicken his body and deepen the cynical lines running from nose to mouth. The mouth itself, with its circle of hair, was perhaps a little thinner, the jaw more aggressive, but that was all. He was smiling, confident in his ability to handle the situation but his eyes were hard as he searched Leon's face.

'You've grown,' he said. 'When last we met you were a boy. Now you seem to be very much a man.'

'Twelve years,' said Leon. He smiled, becoming the gracious host. 'It makes a difference. Malinda, bring some of those spiced and sugared cakes, together with the Artellian wine. We have cause to celebrate.'

Covis visibly relaxed. Not in his face, that was a mask, but in the way he settled in the comfort of his chair. 'A wonderful girl,' he said, as Malinda headed towards the kitchen. 'My only daughter, Leon, and I cherish her.'

'You object to our association?'

'My dear man of course not! She needs someone like you, a person of experience and maturity to guide her feet from foolishness. She is very much in love with you and I am pleased that she is so happy. As a matter of fact I would have no objection if you decided to marry.' He paused, waiting for a comment, and continued when none came. 'There would be details to discuss, naturally, but I am sure there could be no insurmountable objection.'

Leon glanced at Thurston. 'Not from the Family?'

'That worries you?' Thurston smiled without humour. 'The matter could be arranged. Malinda carries no great responsibility and any marriage she chose to make would be acceptable, providing, naturally, that the man was a person of substance.' He turned as she entered, accepting a cake and a glass of wine. 'Thank you, my dear.'

'Daddy?' Covis took a cake, thrust it into his mouth, took another as he sipped at his wine. 'Leon?'

'Not for me.'

'Are you sure?' She stood before him, the tray in her hands, uncertain as what to do next. Taking the tray he set it down.

'You have things to do,' he said. 'Why don't you do them?'

'Yes, girl, do that.' Covis sipped a little more wine. 'Go and enjoy yourself while we talk business.'

'Personal business?'

'Very personal,' said Leon. 'Now do as your father says.' He waited until she had left and then said, quietly, 'You didn't come here to talk about marriage. If you had, Thurston would not be present. He must be too high in the Family council to concern himself with such a trifling matter.'

'To the Family a marriage is never a trifling matter,' said Covis. 'But you are correct. Thurston isn't here for that reason.'

For what then? To stare and check and probe to see if old hurts still rankled? To test his sincerity and make a decision? Leon knew it had to be that. He had expected it and was ready. But he too could play the same game.

'You're looking well,' he said to Thurston. 'Won't you sit down?' He set an example. 'How are things with you and the Family?'

'Well.' Thurston lied. The factories, mines and crops on Elgar were diseased and ruined, gutted and smashed by raids from the hill-tribes. On Hendis the same had happened. 'Why do you ask?'

'I noticed that your stock was quoted a little lower than normal,' said Leon easily. 'A temporary recession, no doubt. It happens.' He took a sip of wine. 'Shall we get down to the reason for your visit?'

'I'll be blunt,' said Thurston. 'It has come to our notice that you are engaged in a business venture outside the normal scope of your operations. You have negotiated with the Jays and –'

'The jewel,' said Leon curtly. 'So Malinda told you about it.'

'She is a good girl, Leon,' said Covis hastily. 'I'm positive that she wouldn't have mentioned it to anyone else. But you can't blame her for having loyalty to the Family. She simply felt it her duty to let us know of the opportunity. After all, my boy, we are practically related and it isn't as if you were a stranger to the Family. I'm not talking about debts, but Charisse and Rolfe did save your life and give you an education. You can't forget that.'

'I don't.'

'And other things?' Thurston was sharp.

'In twelve years a man can learn to put things in perspective,' said Leon. 'But about the jewel, what had you in mind?'

'A cooperative enterprise,' said Covis. Thurston frowned his displeasure.

'I think we go too fast. First we should see the object and then discuss terms. If that is possible, Vardis?'

He brought the gem in a small box of inlaid woods, opening it, apparently not observing the folded paper which fell to one side. Handing the jewel to Covis he excused himself and left the room. From a speaker he heard the words caught by an electronic ear.

'Thurston! This is fantastic! Malinda didn't exaggerate when she said that she'd give her body and soul to own one of these!'

'It is enticing,' admitted Thurston. 'But we must proceed with caution.'

'And lose the opportunity?' A creak and rustle as Covis leaned from his chair. 'What's this paper? A contract from the Jays offering to market the jewels for ten per cent commission. That proves it, Thurston! They never take less than a third. Vardis must have really convinced them to have won so advantageous an agreement.'

'Even so we must be certain.'

'How much more proof do you need? The Jays aren't fools. And you know that he must have a sentimental regard for the Family. Malinda told us how he asked after Charisse and Rolfe. Would he have done that without reason? And he wants to marry Malinda, she's sure of it. If there's anything good going we have a better right to it than anyone else. And we need it, Thurston. The stock is slipping and –'

The voice died as Leon killed the speaker. He smiled, confident of the power of the bait, the irresistible lure of the profits it represented. He gave them a few more minutes, then returned to where they sat. The gem was back in its box, the fallen paper apparently untouched. He picked it up, threw it into the box, shut the lid on both contract and jewel.

He said, 'Would you care for more cakes and wine?'

Covis waved aside the invitation. 'We want to come in with you, Leon. What are your terms?'

'You finance the entire expedition in return for half of what we find.' He paused then added, 'Half the net profit, that is. I'd like to let you have the marketing rights but I've promised them to the Jays.'

'That agreement can be cancelled,' said Covis quickly. 'We can do our own marketing.'

'The division is unequal,' said Thurston sharply. 'I cannot agree.'

'But –'

Thurston waved Covis to silence. 'This is what I propose. A company be formed in which Vardis shall be a stockholder, his holding to be twenty per cent. The Family will provide all managerial officers and hold the rest of the stock.'

'No,' said Leon.

'It is the best arrangement you can expect. Think a moment. You will receive one fifth of the entire net profit and will have no need of concern over the marketing of the gems. More, if you are successful the stock will increase in value so that you are more than likely to end with a much greater sum. You will have no concern over the finance – shares can be sold on the open market once the project is under way. And you will have full command of the expedition, subject only to the veto of a Family member.'

'You?'

'Yes. Do you agree?' Thurston frowned as Leon hesitated.

'It is the best arrangement you could possibly obtain but you do have a choice. You can take it or leave it. Which is it to be?'

'I will take it,' said Leon. 'When do we start?'

SEVEN

The planet was on the edge of the galaxy, the night sky blazing with stars during one season, bitterly empty for another, with only the weak glimmers of distant nebulae lighting the oppressive darkness. It was a bleak world with a yellow sun and a single, bloated moon which hung peering from the sky like an old woman courting death. The seas were restless beneath the impact of wind and tide, lashing against the crumbling shores of scattered islands.

Only the largest bore signs of life, sparse crops hugging arid soil, boats stacked on the sloping beach, a sprawl of low houses built painstakingly of shattered stone. Dominating the island, a massive construction rose like a cathedral, spired and turreted, adorned with grotesque shapes and delicate filagrees, striated with sombre colours and blotched with lichen. A mountain, worn and weathered by the winds and changing climate, pierced with openings and hollowed by countless years of unremitting labour.

'The jewels,' said Thurston. 'Here?' He wore full protective clothing, mailed and helmeted, the ring of hair around his mouth giving him an uncharacteristic pout.

'This is where I found the one you saw,' said Leon. 'Or rather, it was found here.'

'By one of your men?'

'We'd been on a trading expedition. We landed for water and recreation. There was plenty of the first but none of the second and I suppose he got bored. He stole the gem. It cost us a dozen lives.

'We were attacked without any warning and eight were

killed immediately. The others died later from wounds. One of them was the man who had stolen the gem. I found it on his body.' Leon turned, looking back towards the ship, the men and equipment moving about its base. 'That is why I've ordered everyone not to enter a house and all are to stay away from the temple. In this place greed and curiousity can have unpleasant repercussions.'

'That shouldn't bother you,' said Thurston drily. 'Your reputation doesn't lean towards gentleness. Lankis, for example, and Zanobia. Two worlds which have reason to hate you.'

'They tried to cheat.'

'And you taught them a lesson.' Thurston shrugged. 'Well, no matter, I'm not concerned with your morals or reputation. All I want is the gems. Are you positive they are to be found on this world? The one your man stole could have been a lone import.'

'No,' said Leon. 'It wasn't that.'

He led the way towards the beach, turning down a straggling alley until he came to the door of a house. It was closed, with a sheet of leather-like substance hanging loose from the lintel. More scraps of dried and treated skin hung over the windows; the pelts of sea creatures on which the natives lived. Inside, a family sat around a pool of lambent glory.

It was a jewel resting in cupped palms, casting a flood of radiance so that the circling faces shone as if carved from luminous stone. Men, women and children, all with their eyes open, all staring at the beauty of the gem.

'Entranced,' said Leon quietly. 'I think they worship the pictures they see in the jewel, not realising they are the products of their own minds. It is their only pleasure in a life which is a constant struggle for existence. Every house has one, which is kept in a little box set in a kind of shrine. We could take them, but if we did, we should have to fight in order to get away.'

'Gas,' said Thurston. 'We could stun the community with anaesthetics and strip them clean.'

'And what of the temple? There are more people living in that mountain than in the entire village.'

'Gas them too.'

'And you called me ruthless?' Leon shrugged. 'I've thought about it,' he admitted, 'but decided against it. We must find the source and my guess is that it lies somewhere in the ocean. If it does, the fishermen could know where to look.'

He led the way from the shuttered house and moved down to the beach. Men worked on boats which were small and built of many pieces cunningly fitted together. Others mended nets and sails, while a group of women scraped and pounded an irregular square of oily skin. Close to the women, children squatted, spinning bone drills as they bored holes in giant shells.

'You there!' Leon reached out and caught a man by the arm. 'Talk with us.'

'You talk with temple.'

'I want to talk with you. How would you like a new boat? One twice the size of this and half the weight? Answer my questions, and you can have it.'

The man backed away. 'No! You talk with temple!'

Leon moved over to where the women worked. 'I can give you metal blades which will cut your work down by over two thirds. Needles, mirrors, oils for your hands and hair. Soft fabrics for your bodies and perfumes to entice your men. Who will talk with me and get these things?'

A crone looked up, peering through the tangle of hair covering her face. 'You talk with temple.'

'Why can't I talk with you?'

'No. You talk with temple.'

'Morons,' said Thurston as they moved away. 'They don't even understand what you offer. How can people be so ignorant?'

'They're not ignorant. If they were, they wouldn't be alive. It takes skill to farm the sea.'

'Unimaginative, then,' said Thurston impatiently. 'And to me they are ignorant. We come offering them things of value and they aren't even interested. Not even the children.' He glanced back at the workers on the beach. 'Perhaps if we fed them? Gave them candy and spices and bowls of wine?'

'Try it,' said Leon. 'Lay on a feast while I go to the temple.'

It took an hour for Leon to climb to the great opening gouged from the living stone. It soared a hundred feet high, arched, the sides and interior thick with carvings of alien scenes. He studied them, frowning, face shadowed by the uplifted visor of his helmet. Distorted beasts and monstrosities, shapes of facetted crystal, planets with a multitude of suns, vegetation which seemed to be part animal, animals which grew leaves and blossoms. The stuff of nightmare or the entranced mind.

Guards, seven feet tall, garbed like spined and armoured fish, dropped lances of shell and bone across his path. From behind them came a man dressed in robe and cowl of solid brown, his face shadowed, his feet invisible beneath the trailing edge of his garment. A monk or a priest of some kind. It was odd how scraps of ancient religions lingered on in forgotten corners of the galaxy, odder still how it was they almost all wore the same, shielding garments.

Leon said, loudly, 'I am from the ship which has just landed. We come to trade and have many things of use to your people.'

'On Shergol strangers are not welcome.'

'We're here and we're going to stay here until our business is completed.'

'It would be as well for you to leave while you are still able to do so.'

'You'll fight us if we don't? With these?' With his left hand Leon gestured to the lances crossed before him. With his right he drew his laser and fired twice. Razor-edged shells fell to the ground as the guards stepped back looking at their broken weapons, the wisps of smoke rising from the severed shafts. 'Would that really be wise?'

'There are more ways to fight than one, stranger.'

'True, but it is beter not to fight at all.' Leon holstered his gun. 'Therefore I suggest you take me to your superior so we may talk.'

Arcot Tierney pursed his lips and frowned. He was a planetary geologist and a good one, but now he was puzzled. 'I can't understand this,' he said. 'None of the formations I've checked could possibly be the source of any kind of gem at all. I've run tracers out ten miles to sea and fired charges for seismological trace-patterns and the answers are all wrong. Wrong for the finding of crystallised minerals, that is. I'd stake my life that the jewels never came from this vicinity.'

Thoughtfully Thurston touched the rim of hair circling his mouth. 'Are you quite positive about that? There is no possibility that you are mistaken?'

'None.'

And yet the gems existed, he had seen them, so Vardis had not lied. To Tierney, Thurston said, 'Continue your investigations. Perhaps there is something you've overlooked or perhaps the gems originate far from here and are swept over the sea bottom by currents. We have a submersible ready if you want to investigate.'

'A flyer would be better and a complete analysis of a jewel better yet. If I know their composition I shall know what to look for. This way I'm just shooting in the dark.'

'Do your best,' said Thurston. 'At least you can chart the area. Maps may be very useful later on.'

Stepping from the prefabricated hut he looked at the darkening sky. Vardis had been gone a long time and he wondered if he should send men after him. Not yet, he decided. If he was dead there was no need to hurry and if not then delay would do no harm. He glowered at the jars and bales stacked to one side. Not even the promise of a feast had been able to lure the villagers, though a couple of the children, very young, had snatched pieces of candy. Both had been scolded, beaten until they disgorged the forbidden sweets, carried screaming to one of the houses.

A peculiar breed, he thought. Morons if not cretins and certainly lower than the barbarians he despised.

A man shifted to one side, his boots scraping the stone on which he stood. Others showed beyond him, a ring of them around the ship and camp, all heavily armed and wearing full mercenary armour. Perhaps he should have hired actual mercenaries, but he didn't trust them, and his own men should be protection enough. And, at least, they would obey his orders if ever Vardis chose to defy him.

'Sir!'

Thurston turned. A guard was pointing, his arm rigid as it aimed at the sky.

'Look up there, sir! See?'

It was a bird, he thought. It had to be a bird. Then it wheeled, light from the dying sun glowing on its wings, and he saw the long, slender body, the grotesquely developed chest, the arms and legs pipestem thin, and knew that whatever it was it was not a bird. And it was not alone. As he watched three others swooped from the summit of the temple, two others following, then more, until a flock of the winged things circled high overhead, climbing until they vanished, mere points in the heavens.

He lowered his head at the sound of an engine. At the edge of the camp the submersible began to move towards the beach and the sea beyond. It halted at his gesture and Tierney looked from the open turret.

'I'm just going to take a short run to see what I can find. Want to come along?'

Thurston hesitated, 'Have you weapons?'

'Full operational equipment. We'll only make a short survey to check the bottom.' Tierney revved up the engine. 'Coming?'

Thurston climbed aboard, dropping through the turret and sealing it behind him. As he sat beside the geologist he said, 'Did you see what flew off the temple just now?'

'No. What was it?'

'People winged like birds.'

Tierney shrugged. 'So what? I've seen then on Avius, mutations which remained dominant.' He adjusted a control as they neared the water. 'The race is changing all the time. In another thousand years we'll have diversed so much that the word "human" will have lost all meaning. Already we are breeding giants on the heavy-gravity worlds, nocturnals on the night planets, big-eared, big-chested types on worlds with thin atmospheres, and if you want to know just how much the civilised peoples have changed, compare them to the inhabitants of barbaric worlds. The change may not be obvious but it's there. Take Vardis, for example. Have you ever seen him lose his temper?'

'Once,' said Thurston, remembering. 'A long time ago.'

'When he was a boy. But lately? You haven't,' he said, answering his own question. 'It was a long three months getting here and nerves were beginning to fray a little. I don't think anyone managed to control himself, aside from Vardis. He doesn't lose his temper, and you know why?'

'He's a barbarian.'

'That's just a label stuck on a man conditioned by a primitive world, but it will do as well as any other. So he's a barbarian. Civilised men scream and shout and insult each other because they know the other man is also civilised. Too civilised to do anything about it. A barbarian can't rely on that. So he keeps his temper, but when he loses it, watch out. That's when you'd better kill him, because if you don't, he'll kill you.'

Tierney fell silent as the waves lapped higher. He fed extra power to the engine and grunted as he felt the undertow tug at the machine. Switching on the lights he saw a swirl of sandy water flecked with patches of weed.

'There's one hell of a storm going on somewhere out there, and we're catching the edge-effects.'

'Shouldn't we go back?'

'Not yet. It isn't really bad this close to shore.' Tierney flicked on more lights and in their downcast beams Thurston could see the sandy bottom moving as if blown by an invisible wind. The sand yielded to grit as they moved deeper, rounded shingle wreathed with weed rolling past, a bloated something drifting to one side just beyond the edge of vision.

He tensed as the machine jerked to a sudden blow. 'What was that?'

'Driftwood, maybe. Wreckage of some kind.'

'Driftwood? On a planet without trees?' Thurston snapped on his seat restraints and gripped the weapon-controls. 'There's something out there!'

'Sure there is.' Tierney was casual. 'Water, sand, rocks, big and little fish, clams bivalves crustaceans – and seaweed with trunks longer and thicker than any tree you've ever seen. But if it worries you we'll go back.'

He gripped the tread-controls and turned the vehicle, the lights swinging in a wide circle, diffused by the swirling mass of current-borne sand. It was almost like peering into a thick mist, a coiling fog which distorted size and distance. For a moment Thurston felt panic at the thought of becoming lost, of driving deeper and deeper into the ocean until the hull buckled, and imploding water crushed him into a pulp. Then he remembered the instruments and relaxed. Soon now they would ride from the water into clean air.

The machine jerked again, the first blow repeated almost immediately by a second, the twin impact causing the submersible to rock and heel far to one side. Tierney cursed and rode into the movement, the engine whining as he hit maximum revs. He cursed again as the lights showed something long and thin wrapped around a mass of stone, yelling as it lifted and swung towards them.

'Get it! Blast it, quick!'

Thurston's fingers clamped on the triggers and he felt the churning vibration of the heavy machine gun. Bullets reached the threat and smashed it apart, blood rising from the severed ends. As Tierney continued his turn he kept firing, catching a glimpse of a nest of tentacles, a beaked mouth, a glaring eye as huge as a dinner plate. Darkness gushed towards them as the thing backed away, an inky cloud which cut vision down to inches.

'Did you see it?' Tierney sweated as he guided the machine, turning it back on course to the shore. 'The size of it? And the damn thing was intelligent. It used that boulder like a hammer to crack us apart.' He grunted as the machine slowed, the engine note rising in protest. 'It's grabbed us! Pulling us back! Get ready to fire!'

He reversed the treads, hurtling backward until they jolted to the force of a rubbery impact. Immediately he jerked the machine forward, halted, slewed it around on its treads. Lights blazed on a mass of dirty white flesh and Thurston closed his hands on the triggers. A laser would have been better but a machine gun was more rugged, economical and efficient in a medium which swallowed heat. He fired a ten-second burst, seeing the thick slugs hammer into the slimey flesh, the gouting blood, the smashed and broken tissue.

'Enough!' Tierney backed from the lax grip of the tentacles, slewed the machine and sent it racing towards the shore. 'Hell,' he said with feeling. 'To think those fishermen go hunting things like that!'

Leon was waiting when they returned. He stood in the thickening darkness, a vague shape suddenly springing to three-dimensional life in the glare of the headlights. As the submersible came to a halt, other lights switched on, pale floods from the nose of the vessel, scattered glows from the prefabricated huts, all combining to bathe the area in an artificial moonlight. Thurston climbed from the turret and Tierney followed, moving around the machine.

'Look at this.' He pointed to a couple of dents in the plating. 'That thing must have had the strength of a titan.'

Leon stepped forward and touched the scarred metal. 'You met something bad?'

'Bad enough. An octopod of some kind, a real giant. If there are any more like it close to shore we'll have to operate in groups.' He told Leon what had happened. 'Thurston was quick on the trigger or we wouldn't be here now. But what gets me is the way the thing displayed intelligence.'

'It needn't have been that.' Thurston had recovered his composure now they were safe on land. 'A bird will hammer a snail against a rock in order to crack its shell but that doesn't mean the bird is intelligent.'

'Tell that to the snail,' said Tierney drily. 'Before I go under again I want this thing reinforced and fitted with external electrodes. The next time I get grabbed I want to be able to send a few thousand volts into the thing doing the grabbing.'

Leon said, 'Is it as bad as that? The fishermen seem to manage.'

'They've got more guts than I have,' said Tierney. 'Maybe the thing was carried inshore by storm-generated currents or maybe it was the last of its kind, but I'm taking no chances. If the men work by lights we can have the adaptions ready by morning – I don't use this thing until they're done.'

'See to it,' said Thurston. 'Then join us in my hut.'

It was a comfortable structure of insulated metal and plastic, bright and cosy against the night. Thurston poured himself a stimulant, drank it, refilled his glass. He did not offer anything to Leon. He said, 'How did you get on in the temple?'

'Later,' said Leon. 'How did your feast go?'

'It didn't. They refused to eat or drink.'

'Naturally. They suspected poison.'

'You knew they would refuse?' Thurston frowned his anger. 'But why?'

'Because we are strangers and all primitive people have a strongly developed xenophobia. Did you let them see you eating and drinking the stuff provided?'

'Of course not.'

'You should have done. It may not have won their trust, but it would have proved the things were harmless.' Leon looked around, found a chair, sat down. 'You don't know much about trading, Thurston. I do. Before you can get anywhere you must first gain their willingness to listen. That isn't always easy. Then you must eat with them. You'd be surprised how important the breaking of bread can be to an uncivilised people. Then you sharpen their greed and, if you don't make some unintentional mistake or can rectify it if you do, then you're in business. But you'll never make a trader, Thurston. You don't know how to begin. You've just shown that.'

'The feast?'

'No. The way you can't help being rude. You poured yourself a drink and didn't offer me one. You didn't even invite me to sit down. Two things which would ruin you as a trader. I know you don't like me but that isn't the point. You don't have to like a stinking primitive but you have to play the game his way and by his rules. You do it because he has something you want and you're trying to get it from him. Make him an enemy and you can kiss it goodbye.'

Thurston looked at his glass, at the hand clamped around it, the knuckles white. The damned barbarian! He remembered Tierney's warning and forced himself to relax his grip. This was no time to indulge in the luxury of anger but it was impossible for him to apologise. Tierney saved him the need to make a decision. He entered the hut, sat down, held out his hand.

'I need a drink, Thurston. A large one.' He gulped it down.

'That's better. I've got the men hard at work and all should be ready well before dawn. Not that we may need it, of course, but it's as well to be prepared in case we do.' He glanced at Leon. 'How did you make out in the temple? It is a temple, I suppose?'

'It is.'

'Then?'

Leon sat silent, thinking of interminable passageways cut out of solid stone, of chambers and ramps and galleries seemingly without number. Of hooded shapes which trod soundlessly and lights which glowed with the smokey flame of burning oil.

'Speak up!' said Thurston sharply. 'What did you learn?'

'Rudeness,' said Leon quietly. 'I have to keep reminding myself that you can't help being rude. It's the product of your society, the arrogance bred by men fawning on the wealth you inherited. You despise them, which is right, but you make the mistake of despising all who are not of your station. That is a mistake which will one day kill you.'

'You threaten me, Vardis?'

'I never threaten. I don't even promise. Words, to me, are not a substitute for action.'

Tierney said, hastily, 'The temple. You were going to tell us how you got on.'

'Very badly. I was taken to someone of high authority, not the chief as far as I could make out, but someone delegated to handle the situation. He was very patient. Traders are not welcome on Shergol because they will upset the status quo. If we supply boats to the fishermen, what happens when those boats break or need repair? What happens to the skills they will no longer have a use for? If we supply needles and blades to the women to ease their labours, and they come to rely on them, what happens when the supply ceases? The community, as it is, is self-sufficient. Their standards are low, but if we interfere, we will ruin their way of life. The priests do not want that to happen. They hope we will understand.'

'Logical,' mused Tierney. 'But what price progress? And what about the villagers, don't they have anything to say about it?'

'They're conditioned by the temple. The priests do all the worrying and tell them exactly what to do. They must have a system of confessional and a concept of sin. Taboos are common among primitives, some with a basis of good reason, others without apparent logic. Breaking them is almost impossible and we could never reeducate the people to alter the pattern of their lives. In fact, we don't want to. We aren't interested in that.'

'The jewels,' said Thurston. 'Did you learn anything about the jewels?'

'The people have them on loan from the temple. If they are good and obedient, they are allowed to keep them in their homes. If they step out of line, or defy the priests, then the jewel is reclaimed. In that case the whole family suffers, and so there is tremendous pressure put on the culprit to behave. I guess that at times the recalcitrant is put to death by his relatives in order to wash away his sins and to obtain repossession of the jewel.'

Tierney snorted. 'A nice, tight little society. No wonder the priests don't welcome traders. They don't want to lose control of their docile slaves.'

'No,' said Leon. 'They aren't slaves.'

'What then?'

'Raw material. Sometimes a child is born which reveals the spark of higher intelligence. When that happens the infant is taken to the temple, where it is reared, educated and cared for. Later they become priests or priestesses. They aren't celibate, and so by careful selection the stock of intellectuals is constantly raised.'

'Not necessarily,' said Tierney. 'The offspring of intelligent types needn't be intelligent. There would be a lot of recessives and avatars.' He rose and helped himself to another drink. 'They're fools. Don't they realise they are draining the village gene pool of the one thing which could lift them from the slime? The best thing which could happen is for all of them, priests, priestesses and villagers to mix and intermarry. The cross-breeding would work wonders.'

'Never mind all that.' Thurston was impatient. 'Did you discover the location of the jewels, Vardis? The source?'

'No.'

'Then your visit was a waste of time.'

'That depends on how you look at it,' said Leon flatly. 'I said that I hadn't discovered the source, that is true, but I know where they come from. The sea, as I suspected.'

Tierney frowned. 'Are you sure?'

'The walls of the temple are covered with carvings. Some of them must have been made ages ago, and they depict a man, wearing the head of a fish, coming from the waves. He holds a jewel in his hand. Others repeat the incident. Still others are more graphic. The jewel is represented by a star-symbol, and it appears among men fishing, men diving, waves lashing the shore. My guess is that a long time ago the jewels were washed ashore or found in the bellies of fish. They might still so be found. Objects so rare would be handed over to the priests for safe-keeping and they would make them taboo-things, sacred stones sent as an offering to their god. The rest is obvious. To use the gems to maintain their control and so perpetuate the cycle. But, originally, they came from the ocean.'

Thurston stared at the geologist. 'Is it possible?'

'Anything is possible,' said Tierney thoughtfully. 'The ocean's a big place and there could be an outcropping of gem-bearing rock in the depths. Currents and storms would cause it to crumble and the jewels, released, could be swept towards the shore. It's unlikely but it could be possible.'

'We'll have to check the sea-bottom,' said Leon. 'Test every inch if we have to. Is it possible to check the current-flow and get some idea of where the gems may have originated?'

Tierney nodded. 'It won't be easy and it won't be quick but it can be done. We'll need special equipment, submersible working gear, skimmers, armed boats for surface operations and support, radioactives for tracers, sonar, density meters, a lot of things. You'll have to send for what we can't make or adapt.' He stretched, yawning. 'Well, at least we know where to start.'

The sea was dull, leaden beneath the sun, long swells rippling the surface which was broken by little patches of foam. Leon turned, looking back towards the shore. Other boats were on the ocean, the tiny shells in which the villagers wrested food from the sea. Patched sails lifted to aid the paddles swung to the rhythm of chanting, the sound coming flat and uninspiring over the water.

'Look at them,' said Tierney. 'Doing it the hard way.'

One of the other men in the boat grunted as he pulled at a line. 'They'll never learn. I spent three hours yesterday teaching a woman how to clean a skin. My folks were tanners and I learned a few short-cuts in the treatment of hides. There's a knack to holding the scraper – hell, I thought she had it, but as soon as I left, back she went to the old way.' He lifted an instrument from the water. 'You want to take these readings?'

There had been thousands of them taken from three boats over many tedious weeks. Depth soundings, current speeds, the flow and ebb of the water along and against the shore, a mass of data fed into the ship's computer to be resolved into a workable pattern.

'All right,' said Tierney. 'That's enough for today.'

An engine whined and propellers threshed the water, creating a wide swathe of foam as they headed towards the shore. Leon felt the wind in his face, the sharp, acrid tang of rotting weed and decaying bones, the discarded refuse of the village. Another scent caught his nostrils, hatefully familiar, and he leaned forward a little, running as soon as the boat reached the sand. The fire was already out of control. It roared from the doors, windows and roof of a house, living flame edged with smoke, filling the air with the odour of burning.

To one side stood a knot of villagers, a priest among them. He turned as Leon approached.

'Behold the fruits of your presence!'

'The fire? What had we to do with it?'

The priest held out his hand. On the palm lay a kindler; a slug of compressed fuel which could be lit by a spark, the entire unit self-contained. It was a common artifact much used in trade.

Leon picked it up from the outstretched hand. 'This? Where did you find it?'

'The one who owned this house had it in his possession, contrary to the will of the temple.'

'And?'

'Leave Shergol!'

The priest turned to face the fire the villagers clustered like sheep behind his robe. A freak of the wind caused the smoke to waft over them and Leon gagged at the unmistakeable odour. Reaching the camp he made straight for Thurston's hut.

'You've been trading,' he said harshly. 'It's got to stop.'

Thurston looked up from the papers on his desk. 'I don't know what you're talking about.'

'I'm talking about this!' Leon slammed the kindler on the papers. 'A man's just been burned to death because you persuaded him to take it. I gave firm orders that no one was to attempt to trade. From now on no one even talks to a native, is that clear?'

'Are you giving me orders, Vardis?'

'Yes. I am in command of this expedition, subject to your veto. That means you do as I say or you take over. Personally I don't care which way you decide, but if you want me to run things, then you do as I say. No trading. No fraternisation. No contact with anyone unless essential. Understand?'

Thurston rose from his chair, muscle tightly bunched along the lines of his jaw. 'No, Vardis, I don't understand. I am responsible for the economic success of this expedition, and it looks as if the only gems we are going to find are those in the village and temple. I was trying to gain information. That is why I gave the man the kindler.'

'And now he's dead. Did he tell you anything in return?'

'We talked about the temple. He told me that there are many jewels inside. Did you see them on your visit?'

'No.'

'So we now know more than we did before. The kindler wasn't wasted.'

Leon took two steps forward and halted as he felt the edge of the desk press against his thighs. He drew a deep breath and said, 'I'm not concerned with the cost of a kindler. I'm talking about a man who was killed and burned to death for breaking a temple law. You helped him to do it. Can't you understand that we daren't meddle with this society unless we intend to go all the way? A few more incidents like this and the whole island will rise against us.'

'Let them! We –'

'Have lasers and automatic weapons and gas enough to flood the island. True, but what if we are taken by surprise? What would happen to the men in the boats, the huts, those working in the camp? I've seen these people attack and they are like fanatics. They'll lose twenty men in order to kill one of ours. With luck we'd survive, but we'd have to run into space to do it and we'd have to kiss goodbye to any hope of finding the jewels. What would the Family think of you then?'

'The Family is my concern, not yours.' Thurston was emphatic. 'That is why I have reached a decision. The cost of this expedition is already too great, but if every house in the village holds a jewel we could recover the bulk of our outlay. With the gems in the temple we could make a profit. Therefore we –' He broke off as a pulsing note filled the air. 'What was that?'

It came again as they left the hut, a high, shrilling note which lingered in the air seeming to strike resonant chords from their very flesh and bone. A third time and from the village rose a low moaning sound, a wailing, a dirge. From every house came a man bearing a small box in his outstretched arms.

'The gems,' said Leon. 'The priests are recalling the jewels to the temple.'

Thurston smiled. 'That will make our work that much easier.'

Leon remembered the interminable passageways, the countless chambers. 'No. You'll have to forget about robbing the natives. The temple is a three-dimensional maze and we wouldn't even know how to begin to look. They could even bring down the roof and bury them under tons of stone and even if they didn't we'd be at a disadvantage. Lasers don't give much of an advantage when the range is a matter of feet, and we can't keep them gassed for long without killing them all. We've got to find the source.' He paused as another shrilling note came from the temple. 'And we'd better do it fast. Those villagers aren't going to like being without their toys.'

A wind had risen from the east, ruffling the water and causing the salvage boat to rock on its pontoons. It was an ugly craft, a wide, flat deck supporting a mass of equipment together with the bulk of the submersible, buoyancy tanks, a lower deck, a handrail, a box-like cabin on the roof of which were mounted heavy-duty lasers. It looked the prefabricated and adapted thing it was and Leon doubted if it could weather a storm.

He turned from the glassed window as Tierney gave a satisfied grunt.

'Here!' His fingers rapped on a chart spread before him. 'This has to be the place. There's a low ridge running towards the north east with a dip towards the west. Anything in the dip would stay there unless there were unusually strong storms. Then the turbulence would stir things up a little and whatever is there would rise to be caught by the currents and carried towards the shore. It would roll around for a while, naturally, but that is where it would eventually land.'

Leon stooped over the chart. 'Are you certain?'

'Nothing is certain except death,' said the geologist. 'I've run all the data through the computer and had it draw analogs from a thousand different premises. The probability of this point being the one we're looking for is eighty-six per cent. That's twenty per cent higher than any other probable locality and it's good enough for me.'

The radio operator called from the side of the cabin. 'A message from the ship, sir. They want to know how we're getting on.'

'That's Thurston!' Tierney scowled. 'Tell them we're progressing as anticipated and that we will report as soon as we have anything to report.' To the helmsman he said, 'How are conditions?'

The man checked a dial. 'The wind is rising and the current is pretty strong. I don't know how long we can hold this position.'

'Hold it.' Tierney headed for the door of the cabin. 'Let's see what we can find.'

The answer was nothing. The grapnels came up empty and the scoops showed only weed, mud and sand. Leon looked at the scudding clouds and lifted a hand to test the wind. It was noticeably stronger, waves dashing against the bow of the vessel and hurling spume over the deck. At the stern a man was being horribly seasick.

'It's getting bad,' said Tierney. 'Maybe we'd better quit while we have the chance.'

'No,' said Leon. 'We won't quit. I'm going down.'

It was like entering another world, a quiet place of peace and buoyant comfort, almost like space, except that space was full of emptiness, and the sea was far from that. As he fell, locked in the articulated armour of his suit, tiny fish swam up against his faceplate, nibbled at his joints, darted away as he gestured with his hands. Half-way to the bottom it grew dark and he switched on his lights, continuing to descend and watching the blazing colour entering his beam, goggle-eyes above gaping jaws, small predators of the depths.

From his phone Tierney said, 'Are you all right, Leon?'

'Fine. You?'

'I've just got the feel of this thing. I'll be with you in a minute.'

Lights shone from above as the submersible headed for the bottom, nose down. Bubbles exploded from the ballast tanks as Tierney trimmed the buoyancy, the squat machine tilting to an even keel. Leon caught a glimpse of his face beyond the observation port, the profile of the man beside him. Kicking and waving his arms, he moved to one side, continuing to fall with silent grace.

From the phone in his helmet he heard a grunt, the creak of springs and Tierney's voice as he spoke to his companion. 'We've landed. See anything your side?'

'Nothing.'

'Keep looking. I'll swing in a tight circle. If you see anything don't waste time telling me. Leon?'

'Here.'

'Try and land in the field of the lights. If anything comes for you we can take care of them. Right?'

'Right.'

Leon moved a little more to one side away from the submersible. Tierney's plan of defence was probably a good one but he preferred his own. The vibration of the machine's engines could easily attract the very type of life they were afraid of. Drifting soundlessly in the waters he would escape detection while remaining mobile.

He felt an impact and spun, wheeling, recognising a submarine current which ran like a river through the lower depths. It carried him a hundred yards to one side before he dropped below it and swam back to his original position. He could see the lights of the submersible clearly now, a wide fan of radiance reflecting from the ooze of the bottom. As he watched it moved in a tight circle, straightened, headed east towards the ridge. As he touched the bottom the machine was inching up a gentle slope towards a mass of rock striated with glowing colours, shining in the lights like a rippled sheet of mother of pearl.

'Tierney!' he called sharply. 'Halt!'

The lights became stationery. 'Something wrong, Leon?'

'That thing in front of you. Back away from it.'

'It's dangerous?'

'It looks like a giant bivalve to me. Move back, slowly.'

He felt the vibration as the treads clawed at the bottom, the sudden change in note, and saw the lights tilt to illuminate the lower shell of the giant clam. The entire machine rose as something lifted beneath it, mud swirling to blur details. Tierney's voice was harsh in his helmet.

'God! What the hell's happening? We're falling right into that thing!' And then, 'Fire, damn you! Blast it with everything you've got!'

The hammer of the machine guns was a dull reverberation. As the upper shell snapped down, sparks seared from the electrodes, dying almost immediately as the great plates of calcium crushed them to the plating. Leon heard a straining creak, a wordless cry and then a horrible tearing sound followed by silence. For a second the lights continued to blaze and then they too died.

Adjusting his buoyancy tanks, Leon drifted upwards, halting his progress well above the bottom, swimming to where the submersible had last been. In the beam of his light he saw the crushed and twisted wreckage, the thin streams of blood rising from the trapped and broken bodies. There was nothing he could do, and the creature which had risen beneath the machine could soon return, attracted by the scent of food.

He moved on, reaching the summit of the ridge and dropping to examine the western side. He found nothing but mud and shells and shards of stone. The bottom fell and he knew that he must be in the charted dip. He dropped towards it, hands extended, light throwing a patch of brilliance before his eyes.

Nothing. No answering shimmer from heaped jewels or gleams from facets embedded in stone. He searched the entire area, once dropping incautiously low, managing to dodge the snap of shells just in time. A fish swam out of the murk, a third of its length jaws armed with triple rows of teeth, fins and tail like a whip and razors. It was over a yard long and the blow of its snout threw him off balance. It snapped at his arm and he heard the transmitted grate of teeth and then it was gone, heading for the scent of blood. Following it, first in individual clusters then in a solid mass, came the others of the school. Leon rose, fighting to avoid them, buffetted and disorientated as they pounded him with their solid mass. An eddy of moving water caught him, sent him spinning to the east, towards the ridge rearing from the bottom. He hit painfully hard and was immediately blinded by a rising plume of disturbed mud.

As he rose a claw reached from the darkness and closed about his waist.

The rest of the crustacean followed, spindle legs and antennae, eyes on slender stalks, the mate of the claw which gripped him swinging towards his helmet, the whole creature shining a metallic blue in the beam of his light. The brightness bothered it. It backed, seeking to drag him beyond the summit of the ridge down to the lower slopes on the east. As his feet left the mud Leon snatched at one of the two guns hanging at his waist. A trail of fire led from it to explode in eye-searing brilliance against the head of the creature, the incendary thermite charge eating through the natural armour into the soft flesh below. He fired again, a third time, the rocket projectiles reaching to the hinge of the claw which held him fast. Pain caused the serrated jaws to tighten and he felt the armour yield, the bent metal squeezing cruelly into his sides.

He fired twice more and then was spinning through the water, flung by the dying reflexes of the crustacean, a blur of light and darkness stinging his eyes. He landed face down, his faceplate ringing as it hit something hard. He lifted himself, and fell again, slipping down a slimed mass of rock, armour grating, hands numb from the impact of many blows. He felt ungainly and awkward and guessed that the jaws had ruptured a buoyancy tank. If more than one had been broken he was as good as dead.

Fumblingly he checked, reading the instruments on the tiny panel above his faceplate, feeling with numbed hands at the dented armour. One tank was burst, the others bent but still functioning. By shedding all excess weight he would just be able to make the surface.

Pulling up his legs he rose to his knees and stayed for a moment on all fours. Beneath his hands he felt a hard roundness as of massed pebbles and as mud plumed from beneath his hands his eyes narrowed at a sudden brilliance. He dropped lower taking a short, thick tube from the pouch at his chest. He pressed the end to the sea bed and pressed the release. The charge drove the dart deep into the bottom, a second charge spreading the barbs to hold it tight. A touch and chemicals released gases to inflate the buoy which went streaking upwards. Leon followed it, dropping weights, pouch, guns, knife and everything but his armour into the ooze.

Above, the sea had risen, waves chopping at his helmet as it broke the surface. He clutched the buoy and waved with his other arm. The boat came towards him, and a man, bolder than the rest, jumped overboard with a rope. Pulled on the deck, helpless to do anything more than stare at the sky, Leon felt hands busy removing the helmet. As it came free he gasped, 'Mark this spot. Lower a radio-sonde. Then you can call the ship and tell Thurston I've found what he's looking for.'

He coughed and wiped his mouth, looking at the blood on

his wrist. Internal injuries, he guessed, from the the grip of the claw.

'Tell him I've found the source of the jewels.'

EIGHT

She sat cradling a pool of effulgence, the light glowing from her face and hair, touching the skin and tresses with a rainbow spectrum which gave her the appearance of a painted goddess or a dreaming idol as she sat cross-legged on the bed.

From the door Covis Dee Strenach looked at his daughter. More and more now it seemed he found her engrossed with the jewel, sitting blank-eyed, unhearing, unheeding, lost in a world of her own imagination. He crossed the room towards her and rested his hand on her shoulder. Beneath the skin the bones were sharply prominent.

'Malinda!'

She made no response and he had the conviction that if he thrust a needle into her flesh the result would have been the same. Dropping his hand, he scooped the jewel from her linked palms and snapped the fingers of his free hand before her face.

'Malinda!'

She blinked. 'Daddy! What are you doing here?'

'We had an appointment for an hour ago. When you didn't keep it I grew worried. Is everything all right?'

'Of course it is. And the appointment is for tomorrow.'

'Today.'

'Is it?' She frowned then shrugged. 'Oh, well, time flies. But not to worry. Pour yourself a drink while I get ready.'

He wandered about the apartment as she showered, touching things, his heavy face thoughtful. Robots had kept the place clean but the air seemed stale, and even though it was early afternoon the curtains were still drawn. He went into the kitchen and checked the deep freeze and refrigerator. Both held ample supplies of food. Returning to the living room he drew aside the curtains and poured himself a drink. As he sat down he looked at the jewel still clutched in his hand.

Odd, he thought, the fascination they had for women. The demand had been fantastic and the profits incredible. It was a pity the supply was limited, but at least it kept the price high. Too high, perhaps. Almost every woman in the Family owned one and the amount of locked-up capital was enormous. Yet there had been ample to supply the free market as well.

He turned it in his hand, light from the window catching the facets, the inner node of brilliance expanding so that his hand was lost in the eye-catching radiance. A woman smiled at him from the centre of the glow, young, golden haired with the mouth of an angel. Clarmet? Cheryl? Chloe! What had made him think of her?

Dreaming, he leaned back, thinking of years past when his waist had been slimmer than it was now and the universe was a place of untasted delights. Chloe! A party-girl who had fallen in love with him, or so she had claimed, but there had been no doubt that he had fallen in love with her. For three delirious months they had wandered the lush valleys of a fertile world rich with blooms and wonderful fruits, camping, staying with gentle, understanding people, swimming naked in ponds filled with colourful fish. A holiday he would never forget.

'Daddy!' He heard the voice as though it came from far away. 'Daddy!'

'What?' He blinked and saw Malinda stooped over him, her face inches from his own. 'I didn't hear you. I was thinking, I guess.' He reached for his glass and swallowed the brandy. 'Have you been eating lately?'

'Of course I have. Why?'

'You're looking thin.' His eyes searched her face. 'Haggard, almost. When did you eat last?'

'Yesterday,' she said vaguely. 'I think. I'm not sure, but

what does it matter? I'm healthy enough.' She reached for the jewel. 'Please, Daddy.'

For a moment he felt impelled to keep the gem, to take it from her and never give it back. Then he saw her expression and knew that if he kept the jewel he would lose his daughter.

'Isn't it beautiful?' she said as he handed it over. 'You were so good to get it for me. But Leon should have given me one. After all, he did find them and we're rather close.'

'You were close,' he corrected. 'You haven't seen Vardis for months.'

'Now you're being stupid,' she said irritably. 'We were together only a few days ago. When he returned from that planet where he found the jewels.'

'That was months ago.'

'Was it?' She frowned, uncertain. 'It doesn't seem that long. Anyway, he could have given me a jewel instead of making you buy one.'

'He could have bought you one,' he admitted, 'but he couldn't have got one free. Everything found had to be handed over to the company, and he was pretty badly hurt when they got him back to the ship. Thurston had to take over the operation and Vardis never went back to the site. In fact he stayed under emergency medication until they left. Anyway, it's just as well for you not to be obliged to him. You don't want to marry him now, do you?'

Malinda hesitated. 'I don't know,' she said slowly. 'I'm not sure that I want to marry anyone now. I don't think I ever shall.'

'You will,' he said a little too forcibly. 'When the right man comes along.' He glanced at the jewel. 'Now put that thing away and let's get to the meeting. You've got Vardis's proxy? Good. That's all we need.'

The meeting went as arranged, the present officers being re-elected without opposition, the dividend settled, the policy reaffirmed. As drinks and snacks were brought in for the comfort of those attending, Covis moved among the other directors, leaving Malinda to her own devices. A man nodded in her direction.

'Glad to see you brought your girl along, Covis. Has she been ill?'

'No.'

'I wondered if she had.' Keith was a gossip, but he meant well and his son was interested in Malinda. 'Saul hasn't seen her about lately and she looks a little peaked. You want to warn her about overdoing the slimming diets. A woman needs a layer of fat if she hopes to remain attractive.'

'Like Georgette?' Covis was being spiteful, Keith's wife was notorious for her bulk.

'A man could do a lot worse,' said Keith. 'Jarl? Can you spare a minute?'

He bustled off and Covis joined a small group deep in conversation.

'. . . got it from a good authority,' a man was saying. 'Personally I feel sorry for the poor woman. To bear a mutant is bad enough at any time but they'd really worked hard to get a child and when it arrives it's a monster.'

'Stillborn?' a man asked.

'What difference? It's dead now and they have it all to do again. A thing like that hasn't happened in their Family for over three decades and the biotechs swore that the genes were viable and the chromosomes undamaged. It just goes to show that you can never tell. They're suing, of course, but that doesn't do anything to replace the baby.'

'Who was it?' asked Covis.

'One of the Kays. Sigrid Kay Drammen. That's in confidence, naturally.'

'You know I don't talk, Greg.'

One of the others said, 'What made you ask, Covis?'

'No reason, just that I'm curious, I guess.' Covis hesitated and then said 'Have any of you wives or daughters who own a jewel?'

'Wrong question,' said Berne. He was the company accountant, a minor member of the Family who had been pleased to get the job. 'You should have asked who hasn't? The answer is no one. The women went mad for the things as soon as they saw them. More curiosity?'

'You could call it that. Have any of you noticed anything odd lately? About the women, I mean. Things like lapses of memory, vagueness, loss of appetite, reluctance to go out and meet people?' Covis decided to be frank. 'I'm worried about Malinda. She seems different lately, and keeps staring at that damn jewel. I wondered if she was unique, or if others showed the same signs.'

'I'm not sure,' said a man slowly. 'But now I come to think of it, Adrienne has been acting odd during the past few weeks. Locks herself in her room for hours at a stretch and can never get a meal ready on time. If it wasn't for the servomechs I'd go hungry more often than not.'

'You should take Malinda to see a doctor,' advised Greg. 'Young girls get fanciful ideas. She should get married and have some children, that would keep her occupied. Wasn't she strong on Vardis at one time?'

'That's over.'

'Him or her?'

'Her.'

'That's just as well,' said a man at Covis's side. 'I never did trust that man. He always seemed too wrapped up in himself. Did you know that he'd sold his stock?'

'He couldn't,' said Covis. 'Malinda holds his proxy.'

'The transfer takes effect at midnight. We use the same broker and he thought I should know. It'll cost me a couple of commissions but I'll write that off against the company. Right, Berne?'

'I guess we can afford it,' said the accountant. 'Who bought it?'

'Some speculator, I imagine. His name didn't mean anything.'

'He could have been a cover for one of the Families.' Berne

frowned. 'But why would Vardis want to sell? The dividend's high and the stock increasing in value every day. He must have been crazy to get rid of it.'

'Maybe he can't bear to hang around, now that Malinda's rejected him,' suggested Greg. 'It must have hurt his pride, and a man like Vardis couldn't stand that. Anyone know where he is now?'

No one knew and, as far as Covis could tell, no one cared.

The picture was always the same, flames and smoke and a half-seen figure, mercifully undetailed. The rest was memory, the screams and shouts and roaring fires, the wind, the arms clamped around his body, the terrible helplessness. Leon closed his eyes, letting the jewel drop from his hand, not feeling the impact as it struck his thigh.

From across the room Rolfe said, 'Leon, my boy! It's good to see you!'

He had changed as they both had changed, but where the years had given him strength, they had given Rolfe Dee Bouchet weakness. He stood in the entrance to the room, frail, hair a thin cover for his wrinkled scalp, his hand trembling a little as he extended it in greeting. Leon took it, pressed it, let it fall.

'It's been a long time,' he said. 'I was sorry to learn about Charisse.'

'She never forgave me. For years I could read it in her eyes, the reproach, the pain. I killed her, Leon. I sent you away and I killed her.'

Leon turned from the sight of the eyes misted with tears. Beyond the window sprawled a small farm, green fields dotted with grazing cattle, white gates in white fences, neat ricks glowing golden brown in the summer sun. A toy for a rich man to amuse himself with during the years of his retirement.

'You found me dying,' he said. 'A boy of fourteen. You saved my life when you could have let me die. Did you ever, for one moment, stop to realise the implications of your act?

The responsibility you accepted? Or was I just a whim, a gesture to please your wife, a surrogate for the child she didn't have? A pet, Rolfe? A toy? Is that how you regarded me?'

'No, Leon! It wasn't like that!'

'And then, when you grew tired of me, you sent me away. Only you didn't do it. You gave Thurston the job. Why, Rolfe? Didn't you have the courage to face me?' He turned from the window. 'You face me now. Why, Rolfe? Why did you do it?'

'I don't know. I was a little crazy, I guess. Charisse –' Rolfe swallowed, his throat working. 'She loved you. Not as a mother, but as a woman. She loved you and I was afraid. But I lost her just the same.'

'You didn't trust her,' said Leon flatly. 'You asked for all you got.'

'I loved her!'

'You loved yourself, your own, sweet, safe little life. You wanted everything your way. Well, you've got it. Does it make you feel proud?'

Bouchet straightened, some of his lost strength returning to square his shoulders. 'You hate me,' he said wonderingly. 'You really hate me.'

'You'll never know how much. There were times when I dreamed of killing you. You and Thurston and – others. And the worst part was that you didn't realise what you had done. You still don't. By saving my life you became responsible for what I did. Because of you a woman died, a child, my son. And after that many others who would now be alive but for you. You and your damned Family!'

'You're ill!' Rolfe lifted his hand and wiped his face and stared at the sweat on his palm. 'Leon, there's something wrong with you. It isn't natural for a man to hold a grudge for so long. And you can't blame me for what happened on Pharos. Nor for what you did on other worlds. I saved your life, remember? I saved your life.'

'And gave me over two decades of misery. You –' Leon

broke off, looking at his hands, the jewel glistening on the floor. From outside came the sound of an engine and a hover-car came over the fields from where the tall shapes of vessels stood against the sky. 'You sent for them?'

'I had to, Leon. The Family –'

'Comes first, last and all the time. The Family.' Leon's laugh was a snarl. 'God help the Family!'

Thurston entered first, Covis just behind him, both betraying their rage. Walking up to Leon, Thurston said, 'You bastard! You filthy, stinking barbarian! You knew all the time!'

Leon said, softly, 'Of course.'

'You did it deliberately!' Covis was almost crying with anger. 'For God's sake! What kind of a thing are you?'

'Ask Thurston. He knows.'

'You should be killed! Burned like the savage you are. Destroyed as your mother was and for the same reason. You aren't human! You're vile! You –'

Covis choked as Leon's hand took him by the throat. He struggled, veins purpling on his forehead, hands weakly pawing the air. For a long moment Leon held him and then, with a contemptuous jerk, threw him back so that he staggered, and would have fallen had he not slammed his beefy shoulders against the wall.

'Enough!' Rolfe stepped between them, a pathetic figure in his obvious weakness. 'I will not tolerate violence in my house. Thurston! Control yourself. Covis what is all this about?'

'He's ruined us, that's what. Ruined the Family. My God, Bouchet, you should have let him die!'

'Ruined the Family?' Rolfe stared his puzzlement. 'But how? It isn't possible.'

'Unfortunately it is.' Thurston forced himself to be calm, to master his rage and keep it safely under control. He would kill the barbarian, but not just yet. Later, when there could be no question of retribution, and slowly, so that he would have time to regret. 'He did it with that!'

He stooped and picked the jewel from the floor, held it for a moment, then hurled it with the full force of his arm at Leon's face. The smack as it met the uplifted palm sounded strangely loud.

'It was bait,' continued Thurston. 'A lure to snare our co-operation. He didn't tell us, and we didn't realise, that it was poisoned.'

'They're suing us,' said Covis. 'Every woman who owns a jewel is suing us. We can't even begin to meet the damages.'

'But under company law you are safe,' protested Rolfe. 'Your liability is limited. It –'

'The company was formed on Moris under their laws,' said Thurston grimly. 'I was against it but had no choice in the matter. Therefore we do not have limited liability. Also the companies concerned were Family-directed and many of the suits are against individuals. We –'

'Were too clever,' interrupted Leon harshly. 'You swallowed the bait of the agreement I'd won from the Jays. You saw the jewel and realised its value, but even then you couldn't be fair. You offered me stock in the operating company and thought I was too stupid to realise that my share would come only after all expenses had been paid, the officers given their fees, the directors their remuneration. And it didn't end there. The operating company sold the jewels to a holding company who sold them in turn to a retailing outlet with a high increase in the value each time. But I could only get a fifth of the original net profit which was kept deliberately small. And then you made your biggest error. You sold them via members of your Family, and the law on retail is everywhere the same. The man who takes the profit also takes the responsibility. Add that to the commercial laws governing all companies founded on Moris and you're in real trouble.'

'I don't understand,' said Rolfe. 'What trouble?'

'You have no daughters,' said Covis bitterly, 'no wife, so

you wouldn't know. Not yet, thought it will be all over the galaxy soon. Malinda is a catatonic. So is the wife of Greg Dee Fishwan, the daughter of Keith Dee Elton, almost every woman in the Family. And there's more than that. The biotechs swear that the damn things are responsible for the outbreak of mutations plaguing every woman who owns a jewel. And he knew it would happen! He knew!'

'I knew,' admitted Leon. 'And so would Thurston, had he used his brains and eyes. The evidence was before him every second we were on Shergol, but he didn't want to see it. All he could think about was money.' He threw the jewel into the air and caught it as it descended. 'Do you remember how we talked on Shergol? How I warned you that if you continued to despise all those you considered beneath you it would be a fatal error? You've made it, Thurston. You're as good as dead.'

Rolfe shook his head. 'A mental illness caused by wearing a jewel? Mutations caused by a pretty gem?'

'Not wearing it, looking into it.' Leon held out his hand, the jewel glowing on his palm as if he held a mass of trapped rainbows. 'We've known for centuries that certain mind-expanding drugs can cause damage to the chromosomes. We also know that hypnosis carried to a certain point can alter the objective reality experienced by the subject. Somehow this thing does both. It takes a strong mind to resist the temptation to look into it, to see the pictures within the colours, and what rich, spoiled, pampered woman has a strong mind? Boredom curiosity, the desire to stimulate a jaded appetite or the simple need of a novel experience is stimulus enough. The things cost money, and so only the rich could afford them and always the wealthy need entertainment. So they looked into their jewels – and looked – and kept looking until the real world turned into a dream and happiness could only be found in their expensive toys.

'You saw it on Shergol,' he said to Thurston. 'You stood with me outside that house and you saw the entire family entranced. But they had learned to live with the jewels, at the cost of who knows how many lives? To your women they were new, and no one could have any resistance or painfully acquired immunity. And you saw the winged creatures flying from the temple. Mutations, of course, what else? Even the sea beasts were a warning. Monstrously huge distortions of normally small creatures. You saw the evidence, but you didn't want to understand it. Now your Family has to pay.'

'Revenge,' said Thurston bitterly. 'All these years you've nursed the desire to be avenged. Barbarian! What civilised man would do that?'

Leon tossed the jewel so that it glinted in the air.

'If you hated me so much, then why didn't you kill me?' You had chances enough on Shergol.'

'I thought of it,' admitted Leon. 'Often. But I decided against it. You'll suffer more this way. As you will,' he said to Rolfe. 'To kill you would be to do you a favour.'

'Please, said Covis. 'Malinda. She loved you. Is there nothing you can do?'

'No.'

'And you feel no guilt?'

'What guilt?' said Leon. 'You gave her the jewel, not I.'

He looked at it, where it lay in his palm, knowing what it was, what it had to be. An artifact powered by some unguessed source, reaping energy, perhaps, from the very contact with flesh. A toy to beguile the natives. Trade goods. Beads for barter. Lost or mislaid or simply dumped into the sea where he had found them lying in a great heap against the ridge. Discarded by visitors from some other part of the galaxy or from another galaxy far away. Baubles which he had used to serve his purpose.

As he would use the store of radioactives lying in the hold of his ship. The lethal dust which could be spread over a world.

He tossed the jewel again, then threw it to Rolfe, who caught it and looked wonderingly at the giver.

'For you,' said Leon. 'A gift to amuse your declining years. Look into it and see Charisse.'

'And you?'

'I'm going back to where you found me. To the village which burned my mother.'

Those concerned would be dead now, perhaps, or scattered, but some would have survived and there would be relatives of the others, the seed of their loins. They would pay for having killed his mother.

He would burn them! Burn them all!

THE MOTE IN GOD'S EYE

Larry Niven and Jerry Pournelle

An alien space ship, using some motive power unknown to man, comes sailing into the outer reaches of the solar system.

The team sent to intercept it accidentally destroy it, but its course has been recorded accurately enough to extrapolate its point of origin.

A team of scientists, escorted by the most powerful battleship in Earth's space fleet is sent to contact this newly discovered civilization. What they find is at once the most exciting and tragic destiny ever to be suffered by sentient beings.

'The best novel about human beings making first contact with intelligent but utterly nonhuman aliens I have ever seen, and possibly the finest science fiction novel I have ever read.'
– Robert A. Heinlein.

'A spellbinder, a swashbuckler . . . and best of all a brilliant new approach to that fascinating problem – first contact with aliens.'
– Frank Herbert.

THE BIRTHGRAVE

Tanith Lee

Tanith Lee's first venture into the world of heroic fantasy is a big, rich, bloody swords-and-sorcery epic with a truly memorable heroine.

Alternately warrior, witch, goddess and slave, she travels through a barbaric world, sometimes helped, sometimes betrayed by her lovers, searching for a way to free herself from the taint of her vanished race.

'A feast of excitement and adventure . . . filled with rich, alien names, half-sketched barbarian societies, ruined cities, decadence and wonder.' *Marion Zimmer Bradley*